A SONG FOR THE END

KIT POWER

Published by Horrific Tales Publishing 2020

http://www.horrifictales.co.uk
Copyright © 2019 Kit Power

The moral right of Kit Power to be identified as the author of this work has been asserted in accordance with the Copyright, Designs and Patents Act, 1988.
All rights reserved. No part of this publication may be reproduced or transmitted in any form or by any means, electronic or mechanical, including photocopy, recording or any information storage and retrieval system, without permission in writing from the publisher.

A CIP catalogue record for this book is available from the British Library

ISBN: 9798473837742

This book is a work of fiction. Names, characters, businesses, organisations, places and events are either the product of the author's imagination or are used fictitiously. Any resemblance to actual persons, living or dead, events or locales is entirely coincidental.

A SONG FOR THE END

BY

KIT POWER

I'm going to ask you to be precise with your question, if you can. Once it's been asked...

Everything from first hearing the song to now?

Okay, then.

CHAPTER ONE

"Holy fucking shit!" That was Jeff. His brown eyes were wide behind his jet-black fringe, and his goofy grin made him look genuinely gobsmacked – like he couldn't quite believe what had just happened.

Steve was sat behind the kit, nodding slowly. Leaning back, both sticks pointing out from the fist that he rested on his hip – a very Steve pose. "You're not wrong, man."

"Did we get it?" Paul was anxious, hands clasping the top of his guitar. He looked over at Michael checking the MP3 player, a guitar slung over his shoulder.

There was a moment then, when it was hanging in the air. I remember thinking about the times we'd missed recordings because the battery had died or the mic cable had slipped out. Thinking we could always do it again, but also thinking it had been a pretty hot first take and really hoping...

"It's there! It's there," Michael said with a smile, one earbud dangling down the side of his face.

"Plug it into the PA. I want to hear it again," Paul said.

So intense, I remember thinking that. Thinking, too, that he was probably worried about his solo, as per. Thinking that for my money, it had sounded pretty good; loose and powerful, but knowing that he'd be hyper-critical, already straining for another shot, wanting it to be perfect. Reflecting on what a dumb word that was to apply to music, especially our kind of music...

And then the song came back on and we all grew still.

We stood in a loose circle surrounding the small PA mixing desk the MP3 recorder was plugged in to. Behind us, the amps and drum kit sat on the carpeted floor of the community hall that'd been our rehearsal space and impromptu demo recording studio since we'd formed.

I don't know what the others were doing, but I was transported. I'd never felt that way about a song we'd done before. It was like hearing something on the radio and falling in love. It was fantastic.

When it finished, there was silence again. I let it hang for a second before speaking. "I think we've cracked it, lads."

I looked at Jeff first. He grinned at me, face a little flushed. "That's the best song we've written."

More nods.

"I agree," said Paul.

"Fucking brilliant," offered Steve.

"That's the first time I've felt really happy playing one of our own songs."

Michael's statement hung in the air uncomfortably. We'd been going for two and a half years, rehearsed dozens of covers and written sixteen songs before this evening, and yeah, this one was good, but...

"You don't like 'Feel My Pain'?" There was a whiny quality to my voice I didn't like at all but couldn't keep out. "What about 'All We Have Is Now'?"

He shook his head slowly. "Not really. I mean, they're okay, but they don't really float my boat, to be honest. But that..."

I wanted to stay happy, but I could feel my good mood dissipating. Why did Michael have to be such a prick?

"Hang on – you said 'All We Have Is Now' was the best ballad you'd heard since 'Patience'!"

"I lied," he said, then grinned that big, happy grin that lit his whole face, showing he was fucking with me.

Or so I thought.

"But this one..."

"Yeah, this is pretty great. Bill, what was that you were singing in the mid eight? Couldn't quite catch the words."

I couldn't recall. I remembered feeling inspired in the moment, my mouth opening almost of its own accord, the words burning out of my throat without passing my brain first, but...

"Sorry, man. We can listen back to it again if you want, I'm sure we can pick them out."

Steve shook his head, his blond mop falling into his hazel eyes. "No time, man. Gotta get home. Tanya's doing a roast."

We all laughed at that and the moment passed. We packed up, shot the shit, and went our separate ways.

It was the last time the five of us would be together.

CHAPTER TWO

"So, how did it go?" Sarah was on the sofa, looking over the top of our laptop as I walked into our living room.

"Yeah, good. We got a new song written. It's really really good. Jeff's sticking it on the YouTube channel, should be up in an hour or so."

"Oooh, exciting! What's it called?"

"I don't know, hasn't got a name yet."

"Could you sing it for me?"

"I could, absolutely, but my throat's knackered. It'll be up soon, it sounds better with the whole band, anyway. Plus, I still can't remember the middle eight." *Something about flying? Or...*

"How come your throat is bad? You been overdoing it?"

No.

"Yes."

What?

Her dark, exquisitely manicured eyebrows went up, face shifting from warm amusement to cold. The first step in a journey I had no desire to take that evening.

"What?"

Nothing.

"Yes, I've been overdoing it. We did two hours without a break and then another straight hour after Paul and Jeff took a spliff break, and I could feel that it was starting to get tight but I didn't want to break up the vibe, so..."

The words tumbled out of me, no sooner across my mind than out of my mouth. I felt a wave of unease. What the fuck was I doing? And why was I doing it?

"Oh, that's brilliant!" Her face turning to just cold. Step two. "You're going to blow your voice out, you know, if you keep doing that!"

"I know."

"You really want to make a go at it, you've got to look after yourself. It's not just about you boys mucking about - you've got real talent; you've got to protect it."

"Babe..."

"That's why you stopped smoking, remember? To protect your voice. Won't do much good if you shred your vocal cords overdoing it!"

Sorry.

The word wouldn't come. Just wouldn't. I thought it, could hear myself saying it, feel it, but the word refused to pass my lips. I looked at her, face contrite, mind reeling. Trying to say it. Failing. Beginning to panic.

What the...?

"Look, it's just..." She sighed, her brow unwrinkling, softening. "I believe in you, that's all. I hate the idea of you taking yourself out of the game because you couldn't tell those guys you needed to take a break, that's all."

"I know."

"Good."

"I love you."

"You'd better. Go take a shower, you stink."

"I do and I shall." And I did.

***

While I was showering, Frank Evans became the first casualty of the song.

A healthy, nineteen-year-old lad. He was pleasuring himself for the fourth time that day – *Kinky Stepmom Sucks and Fucks Stepson* the Pornhub video promised and delivered – while the YouTube music app on his desktop played random songs. Conscious that his *actual* stepmom, Cheryl, was in the next bedroom over, his usual concession to privacy and decency was to turn the porn playback volume low and have the music high to mask the sound – a necessary concession, his stepmum later confirmed, as she'd been fairly deep into a bottle of vodka, and was, at that same moment, masturbating while watching *Die Hard* on Sky Greats while her husband, Frank's dad, was working the night shift at the sheet metal factory.

The song – *our* song – slipped into the playlist shortly after upload, making the cut by virtue of geographic proximity. Frank was an avid fan of the local music scene and enjoyed listening to his mates' bands hammering away while he murdered fools at *Fortnite* or jerked off to various videos involving suspiciously proportioned and unusually promiscuous women running through remarkably consistent sequences of sexual acts.

This in itself might not have been a fatal problem but for an accident of timing. The song finished and the next track to come onto the player ('Nuff Toonz' by the MK3's) had several seconds of dead air at the start, and during that period of silence, events in the video had happened to reach a level of vigour and volume loud enough to penetrate the thin wall between the bedrooms, putting Cheryl off her stride in a manner most displeasing to her.

As Frank ejaculated into his gym sock, his stepmother angrily banged on the wall and yelled the last words she would ever say to her stepson, voice slurred with drink, "Turn it down! What the hell are you watching, anyway?"

Not wanting or expecting an answer, to be clear, just intending to shame him into shutting up or at least putting on some headphones if he was going to watch that shit, Jesus Christ.

Frank's last action in this world was frantically hitting the mute button on his keyboard, but by then it was too late.

The question had been asked.

Frank's body wouldn't be discovered until the following evening when Cheryl eventually tired of his not responding to her summons to eat tea and stomped into his room, finding her stepson slumped on the floor in his boxers in a large pool of his own congealed blood, gym sock still wrapped around his now-shrivelled genitals.

By then, reports of infection and the events in London meant that Cheryl thought she knew what had happened to Frank, if not why or how.

She didn't.

I didn't find out about any of this until I got here.

CHAPTER THREE

After my shower, Sarah and I watched a film together, cuddled up on the sofa, not talking, just enjoying the warmth of each other. She had assumed her usual position, resting her head on my shoulder. I took breaths through my nose, enjoying the smell of her shampoo; that cheap two-in-one shower gel, deep hit of fennel, delicious. I stole glances throughout the evening down at her straight black bob, framing her pale, pretty face. She was cute, I always thought, if not quite beautiful. I liked her smallness. Made me feel bigger, more manly. I'd really like to be able to tell you I savoured the moment, just enjoying the warmth of her body touching mine, the simple pleasure of being with another person. But I can't.

The truth is, I was thinking about a scene where the lead actress screwed the male lead in a shower and was wondering if I could get away with staying up after Sarah went to bed, play on the Xbox for a bit, and then have a sneaky wank, making judicious use of the a > b function on the DVD player to create my own little soft porn film-within-a-film.

Sorry.

The film ended around eleven and Sarah wriggled into me, her ass moving suggestively against my crotch in that oh-so-innocent way she knew would get me hot.

"Are you tired, babe?"

What I thought I was going to say, with my mind firmly fixated on that shower scene, was *Actually, I'm still buzzing a bit from practice. Maybe I should stay up a bit and...*

"I am, yeah."

The fuck?

"Too tired to fool around a little?" Coy. Teasing.

"Not that tired, no."

"Good."

She took my hand and led me up the stairs.

CHAPTER FOUR

The following morning, we grunted past each other, our usual morning dance of trying to stay out from under each other's feet. Within six months of living together, we'd worked out this was the best way – neither of us are morning people. She hit the bike at eight – happy with the early shift at the shop since it was usually much quieter than the evenings – and I took a shower and got into the car.

Jeff had done his job with the YouTube channel and had bunged out the MP3 on our Patreon page, so I hit the Bluetooth on my phone, turned on the stereo, and let the song wash over me as I drove into work.

Holy cow, it really was good. It was a basic chord progression, sure, and the lead lick Paul had improvised was simplistic, but Jesus, what a hook! I cranked the volume and lowered the windows, treating the crawling commute traffic to our latest creation, and when it finished, I played it again and hit the 'repeat track' icon.

***

I caused at least one death on my way into work that I've been able to confirm, though it seems probable there will be more identified.

Carol Riley had been waiting at the bus stop as my car crawled past, the song blaring, her mind no doubt on the day ahead. She worked at an estate agent's office near the city centre and her dislike of public transport was legendary amongst her friends. A messy divorce, an ex-husband who was always late with the child support payments, a hungry five-year-old, a round of redundancies at her previous job, and an unexpected and very unwelcome change of address to a considerably less desirable estate had forced her to sell the Honda Civic R-Type she still felt teary to recall.

Fucking Kevin and his fucking poker, as she often said to her friends in the several white wine-fuelled misery parties she'd thrown in the last few months.

Still, with nothing going on but the rent, she'd dusted off her CV, put on her war paint, and charmed her way into a job that paid two-thirds of her previous salary with far worse hours. The after-school childcare was also crucifying the budget, but she had a job, that was the thing; it's always easier to get a job when you've already got one. She had plans, as she'd confided in Stacey last night. Big plans. She wouldn't be a secretary for long.

Stacey, who admitted she found Carol a little scary sometimes, sympathised and sold her the handbag Carol clutched to her body as she stood under the shelter. Of course, it was a knock-off, Stacey got the stuff she sold from Mikey, and *he* got them from an actual Bloke Down the Pub, as far as Stacey knew. Anyway, you could tell if you knew what you were looking for, in the lining. But it had been dirt cheap and looked bloody expensive and Carol, fiercely proud, assured Stacey that she would tell anyone who asked that it was a real Chanel bag and fucking dare them to say otherwise. Stacey felt a little stab of fear at Carol's drunk intensity, but smiled and clinked glasses, and then the conversation went back to who was shagging who, who wasn't getting any in her marriage, and if Carol had any new prospects (she didn't).

Eventually, the bus arrived and Carol got on board, showing her weekly pass to the chronically uninterested driver. She scanned the seats, disgust registering on her face as she realised that, as usual, there were no free double seats available, and she'd have to either stand or sit next to a stranger. She'd just made the decision to stand, likely cursing the slightly queasy sensation in her stomach from last night's drinking, when an older lady made eye contact, smiled, and patted the seat next to her.

Despite herself, Carol smiled in return and carefully made her way over to the offered seat. "Thank you!" she said, meaning it, touched, so the lady later reported, by the display of simple kindness.

"You're welcome," the lady (Joanne Robson, seventy-eight and still has all her own teeth) replied, smiling back at the young woman sitting next to her. "It's so mean when people don't make space, I always think."

"You're very kind."

"Oh, I like the company, nice to have a chat on the way into the shops. You working?"

"Yeah, at one of the estate agents." Carol's caution about sharing detailed personal information in public was something of a running joke amongst her friends.

"Well, someone has to," replied Joanne cheerfully, and both women laughed at that.

As she leaned forward, Joanne took in Carol's new acquisition.

"Well, now, that's a lovely handbag! Is it really Chanel?"

Thirty seconds later, Carol was dead.

***

I got to hear the song five more times before I pulled into the car park and not only did the bubble not burst, by the time I pulled the handbrake and turned the key, I was half-convinced we had a hit. An actual, honest-to-God chart-botherer. Even the rough-and-ready mix – the demo vibe – felt right; gave it a raw, real quality you just never heard since digital took everything over.

"Sir?"

I realised with a start that I'd been staring into space, music blaring at close to unacceptable volume across the car park. I spun the volume wheel and the music dropped to a whisper.

Standing outside my car was a six-foot-one ginger male with short, spiky hair and a dose of freckles so severe even the considerable layer of acne couldn't disguise it.

His name was Steven. The other kids (and more than a few of my fellow teachers) imaginatively called him 'Pizza Face'.

"Steven!" I felt guilty, embarrassed, like I'd been caught doing something I shouldn't.

"What was that song?"

Oh, shit.

"It was... I don't know what it's called."

I felt a spike of pain in my head. It was sharp enough to make my eyes water, even though it was there and gone in less than a second.

"... on the radio? Can you turn it back up, please?"

Please. This kid.

"Sure," I said, and did so with gratitude, letting the end of the first chorus wash over me, taking in the second verse, letting my heart rate drop back down to normal levels. I snuck a peek over at Steven and saw an honest-to-God smirk, sans his usual anger and malice.

Astonishing.

I looked away, not wanting him to know I saw, break the moment. I let the rest of the song play out, that majestic middle eight, the killer outro, the held final chord fading slowly. I pulled the key then, not wanting the repeat to kick in.

"Why'd you do that for, sir? I wanted to know who it was!"

"It wasn't on the radio. It's an MP3." *And I'm going*

here why, exactly?

"So, who was it then?"

Dunno, compilation, wife's playlist, something...

"It was my band. The Fallen."

He looked at me for a second, processing, then his eyes narrowed, the smirk turning back to a sneer.

"Yeah, right."

"No, really."

But he'd already turned away, shoulders hunched angrily, muttering to himself.

Probably for the best. I checked my tie in the rear-view mirror and wondered distractedly what the hell was wrong with me. Then I popped the boot, went and got my bags, and headed towards the staff room.

Back to the world of dreams.

CHAPTER FIVE

Kelly was in the staff room already, making herself a cup of that gruesome powdered coffee. I watched the off-brown electric kettle wobbling dangerously as it boiled, wondering as I often did if today would be the day it actually threw itself over with the force of the water movement before the lethargic temperature switch kicked in. For a few seconds, the matter seemed in doubt, but then the light winked out and the lever flew up with an audible click.

"Cutting it a bit fine, Bill," she said, grabbing my mug ("School of Rock", obviously) and adding two more spoonfuls of bitter brown powder.

"I set off on time. Just. Traffic was bad. Worse than normal."

"Yeah, I think there was an accident on Standing Way. Here you go."

She was quick, sugar added and stirred, beverage handed over in seconds. As normal, I used the occasion of taking the mug from her hands to let my gaze slide across her kind, open face and sneak a peek at the hint of cleavage that showed above the top button of her blouse. She had to be knocking on fifty, and what I could see was slightly wrinkly, but they were big enough to hold my attention anyway, and as my eyes moved up to her face, I wondered to myself what they'd feel like in my hands, what her nipples looked like, how they might taste...

"... word from my friend in the union office – Fred's going to be off for at least another month. Apparently, he's denying everything. I can't imagine that he thinks he's gotten away with it. Unless he thinks she swallowed all the evidence. She's a stupid slut, but I doubt she's that stupid. So, anyway, you're going to be stuck with my coffee for another four weeks at least."

"That's great news for me! Well, not about the coffee."

She laughed then, that rolling dirty laugh that, combined with the hint of cleavage and clean soap smell she always had on her, gave me utterly inappropriate stirrings.

"Not for Fred."

"True. He must be having a hellish time."

"Serves him right, the dirty pervert." She laughed again.

I felt my morning glory threatening to return.

"I mean, I know half of the boys in her year have probably stuck it in Wendy Marsh at this point," another chuckle, "but he should have been able to keep it in his pants, especially at his age."

She made eye contact then, and what had been stirrings became a dull throb, all at once. Kelly had always been gloriously indiscreet and one of the few regulars who would give me the time of day, but something about hearing her talk so dirty alongside the sordid nature of what she was talking about... and that hint of cleavage, that scent...

"Bill, you look a little... flushed. Are you okay?"

"I'm... not flushed." *Stop there, that's enough, that's true, that's...*

But I felt pressure growing behind my eyes, exactly where I'd felt the spike of pain talking to Steven, only bigger now. I felt sure it would burst, and I knew that the bursting would hurt even worse than last time.

Then I heard my mouth saying, "I'm aroused. I find you really attractive."

There was a moment or two when the words hung between us. My heart was hammering and I could feel myself sweat. Her face was immobile, unreadable.

Then my mouth added, "Especially when you talk dirty like that and laugh... You have the sexiest laugh I've ever heard."

I saw her eyes had widened, then narrowed, her face moving from friendly to carefully neutral. She went to speak, hesitated, then asked, "How are things with Sarah?"

"Like normal. She thinks I'm a lottery ticket. That I'm going to pay out sometime if she just tolerates me long enough."

I saw that this was not what she'd expected, that she'd been trying to knock me into touch or get me to laugh, and I saw that she was struggling with what to say next, and I wanted badly to intervene, but I couldn't trust myself to speak.

I broke eye contact, took a reflexive sip of my coffee. It was hot enough to burn my lips, but I drank it anyway.

When I looked back up, Kelly's face had hardened.

"So, she doesn't understand you, is that it?"

"No, that's not it. She understands me all too well. She's just pretending she doesn't. Maybe to herself as well."

"So, you thought you'd just come in here and hit on me? Little self-esteem booster?"

"No! Not at all, I like and respect you, I enjoy you..."

Kelly snorted derisively, but I thought maybe her eyes softened just a little.

"...and when you asked, I couldn't help but tell you the truth. I'm sorry. I didn't want to embarrass you or hurt your feelings."

"Then why proposition me?"

"I didn't!"

"You did, you…"

"No, I just told the truth!"

Silence. I didn't dare look away from her eyes, but my peripheral vision still picked up the motion of her chest, her breathing heavy, stressed.

"I'm sorry. I really am. I wish I could have not done it. It wasn't a proposition."

I learned at that moment, for the first time, just how uneasy sincerity and fear are as bedfellows.

"Bill, are you on something? Are you sick?"

"No. I had a brief headache earlier, but… But I am feeling very strange. I don't like it."

She shifted her weight, appraising me. Thinking. "Well, get your shit together. You've got year nine bottom stream in ten minutes. And I have a form register to take."

"I'm sorry, Kelly."

"Yes, you are. Go to class."

CHAPTER SIX

I locked myself into the staff toilet, ran a sink full of cold water. I considered splashing before deciding to dip my face in, immersion. The shock of the chill on my skin made me bring my head up quick and water sprayed over the mirror. I watched the droplets run down the glass and my reflection. The man in the mirror looked scared. Lost.

Is this what a brain tumour feels like? Is that what's happening to me? No impulse control, headaches, delusions of musical grandeur, any other symptoms?

Nope. But still...

Still, nothing. This is the first regular gig you've had since you started supply teaching, and if Kelly is right, there's every chance that Mr Savage won't be returning at all. You are thirty-fucking-six, and despite your repeated and occasionally spectacular attempts at self-sabotage by making awful financial, romantic, and career choices, you have somehow managed to land yourself a seven-year marriage to a good-looking woman who apparently enjoys fucking you, and this job. You're qualified, you know the school, you've been covering his duties. Do the fucking maths. This could be your shot.

And it's way more than you deserve.

I felt a surge of guilt then, rising up so powerfully I thought I might gag. It would happen sometimes; I'd go days, weeks even, feeling okay, even normal, and then some chance remark or thought, or even nothing at all, and suddenly I'd feel the heat in my cheeks, the gorge in my throat. It was horrible, but common enough that I was used to it.

I choked it back. I'd gotten used to doing that, too.

So, stop staring at yourself in the mirror and revisiting past failings like a cliché in one of those shitty pulp horror novels you sneer at Sarah for reading and then fucking devour when she's not around, and get your shit together. Get to fucking class.

I looked at my watch.

"Fuck!"

I went to class.

By the time I got there, at 9:15, the song's body count had reached a hundred. It hadn't yet made the news.

CHAPTER SEVEN

"They set off along the beach in for… for-mat-eon…"

"Formation."

"Formation. What's that, sir?"

"Lined up. In a formal group."

Eye-roll.

"Why don't it just say that then?" Muttered low enough to be plausibly deniable.

On a normal day, I'd ignore it. "Because formation is a more elegant way of putting it. Continue, please."

"Ralph went first, limping a little, his spear carried over one sold… shoulder. He saw things…"

"Partially."

"…partially through the tremble of the heat haze over the flashing sands, and his own long hair and… induries?"

"Injuries. It means his wounds."

Blank.

"He got hurt? In the fight in the last chapter? When they came and stole Piggy's glasses?"

"Oh, yeah, that."

Not a fucking clue. I could live with that, but I could have done without the 'didn't-do-the-homework-and-don't-give-a-fuck' smirk.

"Carry on. From injuries."

Pause. "Behind him came the twins, worried now for a

while but full of... erm..."

"Unquenchable. Unquenchable vitality. It means full of healthy energy that couldn't be put down for long. You know how kids can be like that?"

There was a long pause, then I saw the thing I always look for; a ray of pure recognition, synapses firing, connections being made.

"Yeah! 'Cause like my younger brother, sir, he's a right little... erm... well, he just won't give up, no matter what. Like if he wants something, he just keeps whining and nagging and won't ever give up until he gets what he wants, you know?"

The smile was cautious, careful, and all the more heartwarming for it.

"Unquenchable, innit?"

I smiled back. "It is! Good, Phillip, very good."

A hand shot up at the back of the class. I looked over. It was Andrew Pates.

Shit.

Most of the bottom stream kids were, well, we don't call kids stupid anymore, so let's just say academic study did not play to their strengths. And, of course, I'm being an elitist shit because the truth is, for most of these kids, life was tougher than I'd ever know, because no matter what happened to me in my life, I never had to deal with the idea that maybe my parents didn't love me or the outright certainty that they didn't, much less felt that lack of love expressed by violence either verbal, emotional, or physical; nor had I had to deal with going to school hungry because my parents had to prioritise keeping the lights on over, you know, breakfast. My field is not psychology, but I'm pretty sure in most cases, that will fuck a child up in unhelpful ways. Add in, in many cases, a contempt for intellectualism borne of fear and suspicion (often justified, when you consider what trouble smooth talk and a line of credit will wreak on a family unit for whom twenty-nine-point-eight percent APR might as well be advanced fucking trigonometry) and yeah, it's not surprising these kids were struggling with the prose of Golding, even as they lived out lives that'd make him weep with recognition.

And then there was Andrew Pates.

Andrew...

I think Andrew was a genuinely evil person. I've given it a lot of thought – some might say too much – and I hate that conclusion, that diagnosis, especially of a thirteen-year-old, but it's not a conviction I can shake.

I know a lot of kids pull wings off flies. In most cases, it represents the heights of their pointless cruelty before they begin the passage to empathic adulthood. With Andrew, it did feel like it was just practice.

He was a bright kid, too. That was the infuriating thing. If he wanted to, he could have been top set in everything, an A star pupil. But he couldn't be bothered. He'd rather coast along the bottom, worshipped even by the kids he bullied or ignored, using all those smarts to manipulate the people around him for his own amusement and gain.

Andrew scared me. I think he scared most of the teachers. Any thirteen-year-old that could lie as effortlessly as Andrew was worthy of fear.

His hand was still up. Facial expression the same set-in-stone sneer you never quite got used to.

"Andrew?"

"Why they being so stupid, sir?"

"Who?"

"Ralph and Piggy and that. Why they being so stupid?"

I pondered the question carefully, aware that giving a

flip reply would probably not go well, aware, too, that playing the straight man for Andrew was also usually a losing game, and beginning to feel a pressure building behind my eyes, uncomfortable...

"I don't accept the premise. Unwise, sure, but..."

"Stupid, innit? They know the other side's got all the muscle..."

"...But Ralph knows they need the fire..."

"Yeah, but whasisname is a nutter, innit? And he's got all the other kids all nuts as well, innit?"

"Well, Ralph still thinks the other children will listen to reason, that they will regain their common humanity if he can explain the need for the fire again."

"So, he is stupid then?"

"No! He's just... He..."

I couldn't get the words out. Thinking about Piggy and Ralph and the twins making their way across the sandy beach, knowing what awaits them, trying to verbalise to this rancid creature the awful lost feelings, the hope warring with darker intellect, with the childish optimism that insists all must be well, *will* be well, hurtling towards a date with a smashing boulder and insanity.

All at once, I was caught up, unable to talk. I could feel a lump in my throat. Any second, my eyes were going to start watering. The whole class was staring at me and Andrew laughed once, a single exhalation. Like he knew I was about to start crying.

That's when the bell rang.

CHAPTER EIGHT

It was the fire alarm. Immediately, the class started to pile towards the door, paying as little attention as possible to my shouted extortion of "Do not run!" while still taking enough pace off not to pull a detention.

Smart kids, in certain, specialist ways, I reflected as I followed them out.

Something was wrong. As we lined up on the playing field outside the building, it took my morning brain a good couple of minutes to work out what.

Kelly's class was missing.

I headed over to Fredrick – Mr Hopkins, Head of Year and PE teacher to the core. He was stood back from the lines of kids, checking the clipboards that contained the class registries with his customary scowl, scanning the lines of children to make sure they were all accounted for. I was struck, as I was every time I saw him, by how much the squareness of his head matched the squareness of his broad frame; so much that he looked like a ruddy-faced tackling dummy in human form. The observation was somehow perpetually surprising, refusing to settle by dint of regular observation, leaving me perpetually on edge whenever I had to interact with him.

"Mr Cutter." He held out his hand and I handed him the sheet. He leaned to one side so he could see past me to the more-or-less-(okay, less)-in-line queue of children, and his eyes flicked between the list I'd given him and the kids.

"Mr Hopkins, where is Kelly's class?"

His eyes didn't cease their movement as he answered. "*Miss Andrews* had an incident in her class."

I became very aware of my heartbeat, as though the volume of my pulse had been turned up.

"Is she okay?"

At that moment, I heard a siren start up nearby. Ambulance or police, I couldn't tell. The queues broke out into excited conversation and fractured as kids turned to mates from other classes and exchanged words.

"YOU WILL ALL STAND IN LINE UNTIL THE FIRE DRILL IS OVER!" bellowed Mr Hopkins, in his best 'one more lap!' voice.

He stared down the group of kids until the lines had regained their neatness and the muttering conversations had stopped. It was, I reflected, both an amazing and utterly miserable skill to have developed, to engender such fear in the young. I envied him it, which made me feel terrible.

He glared for five more seconds while the sirens grew louder before, blessedly, cutting out. Then he resumed checking my list with exaggerated care. As he did so, he muttered to me, his lips barely moving, "I believe she's fine, one of the children in her class had an attack or fit or something. Probably drugs. Pizza Face. I think he's dead."

Finally, he made eye contact with me and pushed the clipboard back into my chest.

I turned and ran. The movement of my body pushed the clipboard from his hands and I heard it clatter to the grass behind me. He called my teacher name after me once. I didn't look back.

***

Kelly's classroom was in one of the hilariously named 'temporary' huts that had been put up in 1999 as a stopgap measure for the new PFI-funded Humanities block, the skeleton of which still mouldered behind high 'Keep Out' fencing a full decade after it was scheduled to complete.

Kelly had given me a sardonic and expletive-laden account of the whole sorry affair over lunchtime sandwiches not long after I joined. They were situated on a far corner of the school grounds and I felt winded by the time I rounded A block and the hut fell into view.

There were two ambulances and a police car parked outside.

My timing couldn't have been much better. I saw the stretcher being carried down the short flight of steps towards the back of the ambulance. Steven was strapped to it. At this distance, I couldn't see if he was breathing, but the sheer quantity of blood made it seem passingly unlikely; his face was covered with a sheet, and I could see it staining crimson as they carried him down to the car park, then loaded him into the back of the ambulance.

I moved closer, walking fast but no longer running, aware of the two police officers gathered at the entrance. They exchanged a look, then the taller of the two peeled off towards me, placing his hat on his head, covering his short, blond, spiked flat-top in a well-practiced gesture.

I was still at least ten feet away when he put his palm out and said, "I'm sorry, sir, I'm afraid there's been a serious incident here, I need you to—"

"I just want to know if Kelly is okay. The teacher. She's a friend, she's—"

"Miss Andrews is fine, she's just over there." The officer pointed to where a second duo of officers were talking to Kelly and a group of kids.

The children were sat on the grass for the most part, and as I took them in, I saw a kaleidoscope of reaction; some were pale, some crying, others chatting animatedly in small groups, and a few just sat by themselves, hugging their knees to their chests.

Kelly, I saw, had blood all over her white blouse.

As I looked, the policeman continued talking. "Listen, she needs to talk to our officers now, okay? We have to take a statement while it's all as fresh as possible in her mind."

"What the fuck happened?"

"We don't know yet," the officer replied with admirable calmness. "That's what we need to find out. For now, we need to talk to your friend. As soon as we're done, I'll let you know, okay? I understand you want to talk to her; we're not trying to get in the way of that."

"She's not in any trouble?" I'd meant it to come out as a statement.

"I have no reason to suppose so, no. But as I say—"

"Yes, yeah, okay. I'll... look, I'm parked over there, all right? Can you..."

"I'll give you the nod as soon as we're done. Really shouldn't be long."

"Thank you so much."

"No problem."

I walked over to my car on legs that felt distinctly wobbly. It was partly the unexpected sprint, but mostly that glimpse of blood-soaked cloth covering Steven's head. My stomach churned as the image came to my mind. I opened the door and collapsed into the driver's seat, letting out an acidic belch.

I held my hands up in front of my eyes. They were trembling. I could feel a sheen of sweat on my face. The guilt was back, sitting leaden in my stomach, tightening my throat. I didn't know why, though it seems obvious now.

Being responsible for the death of another stays with you like a scar; and like a scar, it'll ache and twinge at times, that's all.

It was pure force of habit that put that hand back into

my pocket, pulling out the car key, and pushing it into the ignition.

I clicked it forward to turn on the air conditioning. At the same moment, the stereo kicked into life and the song started playing again. I turned it up a bit, just so I could hear it clearly over the fan, then closed my eyes, letting the song and the cold air wash over me.

I had a few seconds of blessed peace where I thought of nothing.

Then a voice said, "What the fuck are you doing, Bill?"

CHAPTER NINE

It was Mr Hopkins.

He was leaning in the door frame, one hand resting on the top of the car door, the other on the roof. I still had one foot in and one foot out of the car, so he was uncomfortably close. So near I could see the veins in his nose, the crease lines in his beetroot-tanned brow so severe they looked like scars, and his bloodshot eyes.

I looked back up at him. "Sitting in my car."

"I can fucking see that. That's not what I am asking."

"Yes, it is, that's what—"

He jerked towards me. The movement was small enough it probably wouldn't have been seen from outside the car, but it was plenty violent enough to make me flinch in my seat.

"Stop being a cunt. You do not walk away from the Head of Year in front of half the fucking school."

I understand, but...

There was a twinge of pain in my head and I found myself saying, "Well, I did, so clearly, I do." I tried to make it sound apologetic, but the words I could do nothing about – I thought them and they came.

I saw his face flush, even under the tan. His jaw clenched. I shrank back a little further into the seat, eyes locked on his, trying to think of a way to start defusing the situation. I felt the cool air from the fan blowing into my face and heard the sound of my band playing in the background, my own voice lifted in song.

"Do you want to hit me?" I kept my tone of voice steady.

"Yes." His voice was thick.

"Are you going to?" Part of me – the part that crawled in my throat hard enough to feel my pulse throbbing – hoped he'd say yes.

"No. The police might see."

I let out a breath. His eyes were still angry, but I could see that hectic colour in his face starting to fade. He opened his mouth and said, "I have never liked you, Bill".

His face was comical, like he was trying to look at his own mouth. He took his arm off the door and stepped back, placing his hand over his right temple. It was crazy, given his aggression of the moment before, but the emotion I thought I could detect on him was embarrassment.

The song played in the background.

On instinct, I asked, "Why did you say that?"

"Because it's true. I hated you from the moment I set eyes on you. Underachiever. Supply teacher in your late thirties. Still in a band. Pathetic." The words didn't sting – it's not like I hadn't known from his cold professionalism that Fredrick Hopkins wasn't overfond of my company – but the look on his face was at once comical and upsetting. It was like he couldn't believe what he was saying, as though he wasn't in control of his own mouth.

I remembered my own face in the mirror from the beginning of the day, after my run-in with Kelly. I sat bolt upright in my seat.

As the song played on, Mr Hopkins continued, "You have a weak, damp handshake. I've never gotten on with a man who shakes like that. Too nervous. And I could tell you looked down on me. Fucking English teachers. Always looking down on PE. Like you're not a lump of meat like the rest of us who'll fall apart if you don't take care of yourselves. Like the shit I give the kids, good habits for self-care, won't have more practical impact on their lives than your fucking sonnets. And you come swanning in here with your lame 'sound and fury' jokes, distracting Miss Andrews, breaking up the routine, all right for you, new fish..."

I felt another bolt of revelation, and before I could stop to think it through, I'd asked, "How long have you been in love with Miss Andrews?"

He took a step back. Then another. He raised his fist. Popped out a finger.

His hand started to shake. His face was now brick red, brow furrowed. I saw his jaw clenched so tight it started to tremble.

"Nnnnnnnnnnnnnn," he said.

Blood started to flow from his left nostril. I saw it run over his chin and heard it pattering on the tarmac of the car park.

"Nnnnnnnnnnn."

"I take it back!" I said, but I knew, from what I'd already felt, that wouldn't work. I remembered the spike of pain behind my eyes as I'd tried to resist talking to Kelly, and as I recalled that, I saw blood gout from Mr Hopkins' eyes.

It sprayed out like a fountain. I felt it fall on my face. It was warm.

He fell to his knees in front of me. I looked him in the eyes. They poured with blood now, more flowing from his ears. As I stared at him and he stared back, he opened his mouth. A tide of blood so dark it was almost black fell over his lower lip and down his shirt.

He held on his knees a moment more, his head now a carnival fountain from Hell. I can't remember thinking anything as I saw him not seeing me.

Then he fell forward onto his face. I heard a splut as his face met the tarmac.

For a few seconds, the song played on and the fan blew air in my face and nothing else happened. I thought. About the song. About Steven. About Mr Hopkins. About my own behaviour, last night and this morning, and the pain in my head when I'd tried to resist the impulse to be completely honest.

That was the moment I worked out what would happen if you tried to push through the pain and not speak the truth.

Then a voice said, "I am going to need you to show me your hands, sir."

CHAPTER TEN

It was the officer I'd spoken to before. I took him in again as he spoke to me, one hand out in front, the other at his belt. Mace? Taser? Nothing I wanted anything of, anyway.

He was tall – comfortably over six foot, I thought – and he looked painfully young to me, his cheeks so pink they looked scrubbed. His voice was calm, his hand steady, but I didn't like the look of the colour of his face one bit; it was almost as though he was wearing rouge on his cheeks.

The song was still playing. I started to move my hand towards the key, to turn it off.

"Sir, please don't. I don't want to hurt you."

I felt a terrible crawling numbness then. It started behind my eyes and spread swiftly down my neck, across my shoulders. I slowly lifted my arms up, palms out.

"Turn in your seat, please. Keep your hands up and out of the vehicle."

I swallowed and heard my throat click. The song was still playing.

"Officer, can you hear the song?"

"Yes."

I could hear running footsteps behind him. More cops, coming fast. Maybe paramedics, too. Fuck it.

He had that same surprised look I'd seen on Hopkins and that heavy feeling increased. I could barely keep my arms up, and impossibly, my eyelids started to feel heavy.

"Officer, I need to turn the song off."

"If you move, I will tase you. I've only just been trained in it, I'm dying to tase someone."

Oh, for fuck's sake.

"You didn't mean to say that, did you?"

"No! No, I couldn't help it." His eyes swivelled to me, real panic now joining that dreadful, adrenaline-fuelled excitement I'd seen before. "Did you do this?"

Oh, fuck.

"Yes, it was me," I said, just as the other three officers turned up, just as the paramedics knelt down over what I already knew was the corpse of Mr Hopkins, PE teacher. "It's all my fault. Steven and Fredrick both died because of me."

There was a moment of perfect silence. Then the paramedics resumed their mumbled conversation and one of the other cops asked, "Could you repeat that, sir?"

I did.

There was another pause. In it, I heard the song restart. I looked at the two paramedics, the four officers, all comfortably in earshot. Next to Mr I-Want-To-Tase-You, the man who'd asked me to repeat my confession was shorter and bulkier, his freckles feeling incongruous on his lined face. The other two officers stood slightly to one side. It was a similar young/old paring, the younger man with suspiciously black hair above piercing blue eyes, the older with a lower jaw that conspired with the dark stubble on his chin to give him a rodent-like appearance. The paramedics, a man and a woman, worked together, muttering to each other, their backs to me.

I felt my arms tremble from the effort of holding them up. My lips were numb.

"Could you explain what you mean?"

I sighed.

"I can't explain it, no, but I know what's happening."

"Describe it to me, please."

It was hard to get the words out clearly. I felt as though my jaw and tongue muscles had been replaced by putty.

"It's the song. Once you hear it, you have to tell the truth. If you try and lie, it kills you."

"Do you think this is a laughing matter? Two people have died!"

"No, it's not a laughing matter! When's the last time you masturbated?" I hadn't meant to yell, but all at once, I was feeling a surge of rage so total it made me shake. It hurt my throat, but I felt some of the fog begin to lift, which was very welcome.

"Last night, I was watching Corrie. I've got a mad hard-on for Bethany Platt."

As miserable and terrified as I was feeling, the look on the officer's face as he said this almost made the whole sorry mess worthwhile.

His colleagues each took a step away, half-turned towards him, their expressions also registering shock, disgust, and amusement.

Then the first officer to approach me pulled a black-handled device and pointed it at me. "You ask one more fucking question and I will tase you. And I will enjoy it. So shut your fucking mouth."

I shut my fucking mouth.

The cops were still looking at each other. For a couple of moments, nobody wanted to speak.

"What the fuck are we supposed to do now?" The freckled cop had taken care to turn his back on me, directing the question at his three colleagues.

"We're supposed to arrest him." Normally, when three people say something in unison, it's pretty funny. Here, not so much. They all looked scared as hell. Even one of the paramedics jumped when it happened.

"Okay, okay. Fuck. Okay, here's what I need. I need to question him. Okay?"

"Yes."

"No."

"Not really, but I won't stop you."

He turned to the officer with the Taser, who'd spoken this last. "Andy, can you please not tase him so I can question him?"

"I won't tase him unless he asks a question or says something I really don't like. Or if I have an involuntary muscle spasm."

He turned back to me. "You know he's telling the truth?"

I sighed. This seemed unlikely to end well. "Yes."

"Good." He took a moment to collect his thoughts. "When did you become aware of the song having this effect?"

"When Mr Hopkins died is when I worked it out. I knew something was wrong with me before that, but I didn't know what."

"When did you first hear the song?"

"Yesterday. I performed it with my band for the first time and we recorded it. That's what we're listening to now."

"And since then, you've had to tell the truth?"

"Yes."

"What happened when you tried to lie?"

"A stabbing pain behind my eyes. As soon as I started talking, it went. It's almost uncontrollable anyway, as soon as I think the words, I say them."

"Did you know the song would have this effect?"

"No! We'd just written it that afternoon, I wasn't even sure it'd work as a song."

"Are the effects reversible?"

"I don't know."

"Are they permanent?"

"I don't know."

"Why do you think the child in the classroom died?"

"I don't know, but he heard the song this morning when he came into class. I was listening to it in the car. So, he must have been trying not to say something, not tell some truth."

"And what did you ask this chap? What truth did he die for?"

I'd been staring at the ground throughout this exchange, but that last made me look up. As I did so, I saw that behind the paramedics and the officers, a small knot of children were standing behind Kelly.

They were all in earshot, of both me and the music from the car. I felt tears sting my eyes as I answered.

"I asked him how long he'd been in love with Kelly."

For a moment, the only sound was the song playing, building back to the middle eight. I had time to realise that I still hadn't listened to it close enough to pick out the words. I started to do so, desperate for any distraction from the slow-motion car crash that was happening in front of me.

Then Kelly asked, "What the fuck is going on?"

CHAPTER ELEVEN

The two paramedics, four policemen and I started talking, telling our own version of events to that point. I'd have found it more amusing if I hadn't been part of the wall of noise. It was certainly interesting the spin different people were putting on what they'd heard; not, obviously, out of dishonesty, but purely from having different perspectives. It was almost impossible to make anything out in any detail, however, due to the sheer din, and my primary feeling was dread. I couldn't *not* talk and neither could the others, and I saw that same horror reflected on their faces; loss of control, of autonomy, over our own voices.

I thought I'd heard something from one of the paramedics, but before I could follow up, Freckles was talking again. "Hey, any chance you could turn off the music so we don't make this shit show any worse?"

"I can turn it off here, yes," I said, reaching into my pocket and unlocking my phone.

I'd set it on silent mode before walking to the staff room, part of my normal routine. So it was only as I stopped the music player, cutting off the song mid-first verse, that I saw the seventeen message alerts from Jeff.

Oh, fuck.

"Why are you pulling that face?"

Oh, fuck.

"Because my bandmate, Jeff, the bass player, has sent me seventeen text messages since I got to school this morning. And he manages the social media accounts for the band. He was going to put the song out on our YouTube channel last night, and the MP3 out to our Patreons this morning. Normally, he messages once or twice just to confirm they've gone up."

"Oh, fuck. What does the last message say?"

"It says 'one hundred fucking K views right now, call me back dickhead, this is fucking epic, we're going viral!!!!!!' There's six exclamation points on the end."

Some of the kids giggled. I glanced up at them, a gaggle of thirteen- to fourteen-year-olds that looked like everything from children to almost-adults. Almost all of them looked scared (and fair enough, they'd just seen one of their classmates bleed to death from his face), but even that didn't stop the smiles at hearing a teacher swear. I remember thinking, distractedly, that this had to be the end of my career.

"Jesus, this is bad." Freckles winning the grand prize for stating the fucking obvious.

Andy-with-the-Taser turned to him. "Seems to me it might make our job easier, actually. What are you worried about?"

"I'm scared to death that someone will start asking us when the last time we broke the law was, and what it was we did. What about you?"

I saw Andy wince before replying "When you said that, I came pretty close to shitting myself."

More giggles from the kids. I almost smiled myself.

"So, we're agreed it's a fucking issue then."

Everyone – Kelly, cops, paramedics, kids, me – said, "Yes."

"Wait!"

It was one of the kids. I looked at him. Timmy... something? No, Tommy. Tommy Everington. Gangly kid, tall but awkward, clumsy. Palled around with Steven, I recalled.

His face made my heart sink. Pale, sweaty.

"So… the song makes you tell the truth?"

This time, everyone – paramedics, police, me, Kelly, and all the kids – said, "Yes!" at the same time, and this time, there was nothing remotely funny about it. I felt my arms break out in goosebumps so quick it was almost painful.

"And if you try not to…" he swallowed hard, then continued "…it'll kill you, like Hopkins?"

Thirty voices, all at once, "Yes."

He burst into tears. "I killed him. Steven, I killed him! I said…" Tears were streaming down his face, and as he carried on talking, I saw a snot bubble form under his left nostril. "He said he actually didn't mind this class, and I said, 'You gay or something?' And he went red and then he died bleeding from his eyes and nose and mouth and ears and it's my fault."

Thunderstruck silence greeted Tommy's confession. Then Kelly pulled him in close, hugging the kid as sobs shook his frame. As she did, she shot me a look that told me that our days of friendly banter were over forever. Given the scale of what was unfolding, that understanding really shouldn't have mattered, but it felt like a stone sitting in my stomach, all the same.

More guilt.

I looked around at the others; the kids, the policemen, the paramedics. Where eyes were looking in my direction, they swiftly dropped, and everywhere I saw furrowed brows and scowls.

I watched as our worlds changed forever.

And at that point, my mind caught up with the word I thought I'd heard one of the paramedics say. I turned to him. "What did you say about quarantine?"

The man looked up at me, apologetically.

"I said, as soon as the second casualty occurred, I radioed in to confirm we had a potential contagion and would need quarantining."

A stunned silence greeted this.

It was Officer Freckles that spoke up, pointing at me. "Okay, you can take me to where Jeff lives?"

"Yes, Stony Stratford, I don't know the house number because it's not on the door, but I've been there and I can direct you there and point it out once I'm on the street."

"Okay." He turned to the paramedics. "How long before the quarantine kicks in?"

The woman answered, "Literally any minute, the ambulances and other police vehicles should be on their way immediately. The hospital is seven minutes away at speed limit, so…"

As if on cue, we heard sirens.

"Okay, rock star," Freckles pointed at me, "you're with me, we're going to Jeff's house now. The rest of you stay here."

"Why?" asked Officer Andy I-Want-To-Tase-You.

"Because I need him to get me there, and the rest of you need to stay here to hold off the quarantine, buy us some time."

"And how are we supposed to do that if we can't lie?"

"Fuck. Fuck! You fucking can't. Fuck it. We're going anyway."

He gestured and turned towards his car. I trotted after him, hoping I wouldn't get ninety thousand volts in the arse before I got there.

I didn't.

As we sat in the car, I turned to the officer. "What's your

name?"

"John. John Cash."

I burst out laughing as he hit the sirens and lights. He looked at me quizzically.

"At least I don't have to ask if you're bullshitting me."

He smiled back without much mirth. "Yeehaw," he said, then he hit the sirens and lights and slammed his foot down on the accelerator.

CHAPTER TWELVE

As we pulled out of the school car park and hit the main road, I saw a small convoy of ambulances and police cars in the rear-view mirror. John cursed under his breath and pushed us forward faster. We hit the first roundabout doing forty-five miles an hour, and the noise of the tyres as he swerved the car left then right to keep us going straight made my head hurt.

"Fucking hell," I said, placing my hand against the roof for balance.

"We need to get some distance on the school."

Just then, his radio crackled to life. "Victor Tango Charlie, we have you leaving Lord Grey School, please advise."

"Base, this is Victor Tango Charlie, am en route to suspect's house, have second suspect in the vehicle with me aiding with navigation." John looked over at me as he spoke into the radio, panic in his eyes.

There was a short pause.

"Victor Tango Charlie, this is base, please repeat last."

As he pressed the button to start talking, I grabbed the radio from his shoulder and pulled. He fought me for a second as he started to talk, then realised what I was doing and relaxed. I tore the handset from his chest, pulling until the lead came out of his vest. At the same time, he reached with his right hand and my window began to slide down. As he continued repeating his last statement word for word, I threw the radio out of the window.

He nodded. "That solves that."

"Is that how they'd track us?"

"That and the GPS in the car."

We looked at each other. John pulled us over into a bus stop and started kicking the radio box under the main dashboard. After a few blows, it came loose enough for him to rip it out and hurl it into the bushes lining the road.

The elderly lady waiting for her bus stared at us both with astonishment. John turned to her. "It's vital we're not prevented from reaching our destination. Civilisation is at stake," he said.

The old lady blinked rapidly twice and said, "Well, then, best of British luck to you both."

We thanked her, climbed back in the car, and John sped away.

The words *civilisation is at stake* hung over me for the rest of the day.

***

Alfie Jones lived on the Isle of Wight and had a Very Online Life. Seventeen years old and a keen music fan who lived for the annual festival, his Twitter and YouTube feeds were always full of song recommendations, and he was both admired and slightly resented in his online communities for his relentless pursuit of the Next Big Thing in indie rock.

His school had wisely set Monday morning as a study period, and Alfie was, in consequence, doing what he loved most: shooting the shit with his friend Rachel on Skype while listening to new music.

They'd both been alerted to the untitled song at the same time as the number of views ticked north of two hundred thousand and agreed to listen to it together while they talked.

Rachel was just finishing her first year at university,

studying criminology, and her own band, Displacement Activity, was gearing up for a mini summer tour of London dive venues.

"I knew he didn't really like our stuff, that's the worst part," she told me, tears cutting tracks through her make-up as she stared at her shoes. "He never liked Goth or Punk, so putting them together… but he liked me, you know? He liked me, and he'd say he liked my stuff because of that. And I enjoyed it because I enjoyed him."

I told her I understood. Which was, of course, the truth.

It was a deliberate tease when she asked him, halfway through hearing our tune, if he preferred it to her own work.

His hands immediately flew to his face, but she heard his eyes burst over the headphone mic he was wearing and saw the blood gushing between his fingers before his body fell from the chair.

"Do you understand what it's like? To know you are responsible for killing someone because of something you did?"

I told her I knew exactly what that felt like.

CHAPTER THIRTEEN

I advised John to park a little up the street. "I don't know how paranoid Jeff is, but he smokes a lot of weed, so your appearance on his doorstep is likely to alarm him."

John nodded. "I really hate arresting people for weed. I'll do almost anything to look the other way. That's not what I am here for."

I thought about other questions I could ask, then realised with a nasty start that I didn't want the answers; not least because if I knew how John planned to approach this, I wouldn't be able to avoid telling Jeff if he asked.

What a fucking mess, I thought as we got out of the car, crossed the road, and rang the doorbell.

It took three attempts before we heard movement from inside the house: a door opening, heavy footsteps coming down the stairs, and an irritated voice muttering loudly, "Okay, okay, I'm coming, I'm coming, I'm coming..."

The door opened and there stood Jeff.

He was wearing a ratty blue dressing gown, open. His chest was pink and almost hairless, and a line of dark hair ran from the bottom of his belly button down into the long black denim shorts he had mercifully covering his lower half. His gut hung over the empty beltline. Half a roll-up dangled from the corner of his mouth, unlit.

He frowned. "Shit, Bill, what's occurring?"

"Well, Jeff, the song we wrote and recorded last night forces anyone who hears it to tell the truth at all times. In fact, it compels them to do so. They can't lie and have to answer any direct question honestly and can only make honest statements when they talk. And if they try to lie, it kills them, by causing, as far as I can tell, their brain to haemorrhage in about a thousand places at once so that blood runs out of their ears, eyes, nose, and mouth.

"I know since I heard the song last night, any even momentary attempt to disassemble has caused me incredibly painful headaches. Officer Cash here, three other police officers at the school, two paramedics, and Kelly and her entire class of children have already been infected due to hearing the song playing on my car stereo.

"While I was in the process of turning the song off, I saw your messages about the YouTube version going viral, at which point Officer Cash decided to break the quarantine that one of the paramedics had called on the school in order to drive over to get you to take down the video before too many more people hear the song and suddenly find themselves unable to lie under pain of death."

Jeff had been nodding through my monologue. As I finished, he reached into the pocket of his dressing gown and brought out a Clipper lighter. He lit the cigarette in his mouth, took a deep drag, and on the exhale, said, "Well, I think you'd better come in."

CHAPTER FOURTEEN

Jeff trailed a line of what smelt to me to be distinctly herbal tobacco smoke behind him as he wandered into his living room. "Either of you two want a cuppa?"

"Actually, I don't really like tea," we said, in perfect unison. Jeff didn't even break stride. "Well, I'm fucking having one. Wait here." He gestured to his living room/dining room/student squat circa 1997.

I took in the empty mugs, overflowing ashtrays, battered-looking black laptop, and vinyl copy of *Dark Side of the Moon* spread out over the dining table that was slightly too large for the room it was in. I took in the sleek, black, expensive-looking stack stereo system in the corner. I observed the giant tie-dye flag displaying a purple yin/yang sign that was nailed over the window in place of curtains. Most of all, I looked at the beanbags on the living room floor in front of the television that were the only seating arrangements in that room. The PS4 controller that sat in the arse-shaped indentation of the beanbag closest to the telly completed the scene.

"Does Jeff do anything other than play in your band, smoke weed in this house, and play on his PlayStation?" asked John.

"Logically, the answer must be yes, but I have no idea about any details or specifics," I replied.

John raised his voice, "Jeff, I need to hurry you, I really want to get this song taken down before too many more people hear it!"

"I'm coming, I just need a cup of tea. I'm not normally up to receiving visitors at this hour." Jeff's reply was calm, even amused, I thought.

"Have you noticed any funny effects from the song, Jeff?"

"No, mate. I mean, I haven't spoken to anyone since rehearsal, but I don't feel any different."

I thought about this for a minute.

"Well, now you've heard, aren't you worried about it?"

I heard his chuckle over the rattling noise the kettle made as it boiled. "Not really, mate. I'm an open book anyway, so it don't make much odds to me."

I heard pouring water and the rattling of a teaspoon in a cup. I thought more. "Okay, but what about other people? We've forced over a hundred thousand people to be completely honest, under pain of death, without warning them or getting permission – and they don't even know that lying is now fatal. Doesn't that bother you?"

Jeff rejoined us, a large, pink mug in his hand. I could see the steam rising from it. "Nope, doesn't bother me a bit. World could do with a bit of honesty, that's what I think."

John and I stared and Jeff... Jeff stared back, smiling.

John spoke next, very calmly. "Jeff, did you know this was going to happen?"

"Nope. Didn't have a clue," Jeff replied, cheerfully.

"Right. Well..." John gestured in the direction of the laptop, "could you get the song taken down, please, so we can at least limit the damage?"

"Absolutely, I can," Jeff said.

He paused.

"But I won't."

CHAPTER FIFTEEN

John's instincts and reflexes were both far sharper than mine. He started to crouch and reach for something on his belt as Jeff flicked his wrist, sending the scalding hot tea arcing out from his cup in our direction. I only started to move after the tea was in the air, flinching desperately and with zero grace away from them both, back into the living room. I saw the bottom of the arc of the liquid catch the top of John's head, but he was already starting to uncurl back up, a small, black canister in his hand.

He was fast.

Jeff was faster.

The hammer came out of his dressing gown pocket like a psychotic conjuring trick, and it was still accelerating in an upward arc when it connected with John's jaw. There was a loud crack, like the sound of thick wood snapping.

John fell immediately, his whole body limp.

Jeff looked at John's crumpled form on the dirty carpet, then at me. "I really didn't want to do that," he said.

Then he brought the hammer down on the back of John's head.

This time, the sound was more like the cracking of an eggshell. When Jeff lifted up the hammer, I saw blood on the head.

"Jesus, Jeff."

He looked at me. "How long before they come looking?"

"They're already looking. We broke quarantine and

dumped the GPS, so they'll be looking for the car and when they find it, they'll send everyone." The words were being ripped out of me, even as I felt tears stinging my eyes. I continued to answer his question through sobs. "I don't know how long that'll take, but I can't imagine it'll be long." I swiped at my eyes and nose, and then asked, "Jeff, why did you do that?"

Jeff looked at me. His face was pale and I could see his jaw trembling. His nostrils were flaring, his pupils large and reflective. His expression was so alien, so un-Jeff, that it took me a second to place it: shock, sure, but under that, rage. Jeff was *furious.* As he spoke, I saw tears on his cheeks and spittle flew from his mouth as the words came through him.

"Because I've lived an honest life and spoken the truth since I was a teenager. Because I believe that one of the main reasons we're so fucked as a species is because of our capacity to lie without consequence. Because I have been the change I want to see in the fucking world for the best part of fifteen years now and all I have to show for it is a string of shitty jobs I can't hold onto and this shitty house I can't even afford curtains for and a weed habit I have to maintain just to stay honest because the world's lies are so fucking infectious, I have to stay baked to sublimate the fucking programming and just *be*. I go on marches and hand out leaflets and tell people how the world is and those that don't sneer or laugh or spit maybe get halfway through reading the soggy leaflet I give them before they turn back to their paper or radio and start pouring the poison and lies and propaganda back into their minds.

"The planet is dying, billions of us are going to die in the next fifty years, and all because the people who run things lie and lie and lie about how bad it is and give the rest of us enough scraps from the table that we let their lies comfort us even as we know, deep down, that we're fucked and they're the ones fucking us.

"And now we, you and I, have created something that'll

change all of that at a stroke, kill the bullshit forever, and it's already going viral, and your response to that is to bring a pig to my home to shut it down. I did what I could for years and knew it would never be enough, and now, now, we have the power to change *everything,* and you're asking me *why?*

"Fuck you, man. I didn't want to do that, and I didn't enjoy it, but I'll kill every pig in this country and anyone else who tries to stop me because it's way past time the whole thing came tumbling down. So, I killed him and now I'm going to figure out how to boost the signal as loud and far and fast and effectively as possible. And if you try and stop me, band brother, I will kill you, too. And if you ask me any more questions, I will hit you in the head with this hammer hard enough that you won't hear the answer."

"People are going to die, Jeff!" It wasn't a question, but it still felt like a risk. I could feel tears coming to my eyes. For him. For John Cash. For myself.

Jeff stared down at me, blinking furiously, and for a second, I thought he was going to swing for me anyway. Instead, he spoke again, and his voice was soft and almost calm. "You know, I have never understood why people claim the trolley problem is any kind of moral dilemma. You pull the lever, one person dies. You don't, five people die. That's not a dilemma. That's not a fucking puzzle. You pull the fucking lever, or else you're a cunt, that's all.

"The song will kill a few hundred thousand, perhaps a few million, the first week or so. But it'll kill capitalism, too. Forever. And if something doesn't do that, capitalism will kill us all. Very, very soon, now."

He held my eyes the whole time he spoke. Even if he hadn't been under the influence of the song, I would have believed him.

"It's just a trolley problem, mate. Which is to say, not a problem at all. Now hush. I've gotta get moving."

I opened my mouth, then shut it again. There didn't seem to be anything else to say.

Jeff slammed his laptop shut, pulled the charger plug from the wall. As he did this last, I heard sirens in the distance.

"Fuck!" Jeff scrambled around on the table, moving the mugs around, lifting up the LP, and spilling the tobacco on top of it over John. "Where are my fucking car keys?"

"On the coat hanger by the front door." I'd seen them there on the way past and as soon as Jeff asked the question, my mind threw up the memory of spotting them.

Jeff smiled at me, that same happy smile I'd seen at rehearsals, at gigs, on stage, when we'd hit a sweet spot with a song. It lit up his face and seeing it there and then made me ache badly – for what we'd been last night and could never be again.

He ran for the front door as the sirens got louder, laptop under his arm, lead trailing behind him. I heard the jangle as he grabbed the keyring from the hallway, then the front door opened. Then I heard his footsteps, followed by a car door, followed by a car engine, accelerating fast, then fading as the sirens grew louder.

I turned back to John. There was a large and spreading pool of blood under his head. I watched it spread across the dirty carpet for a few seconds. I felt my vision get fuzzy, then run grey.

Then I passed out.

I stayed out for twenty minutes.

CHAPTER SIXTEEN

A pain in my left ear brought me round.

Leaning over me was a man in a radiation suit – it looked exactly like Marty McFly's from *Back to the Future*, only white instead of yellow. Behind the dome of clear Perspex, his face seemed kind; blue eyes set beneath a bald head, fringed with short, grey-white hair. His face was lined, but in ways that suggested laughter and thought.

"Back with us?"

"Yes, thank you."

He leaned closer, staring into my eyes. It should have been uncomfortable, but the sheet of plastic between us took the edge off the intimacy. Behind him, I saw and heard more movement, around where John had fallen. I sat up, but the man in front of me placed a hand on my shoulder.

"I need you to lie still for a minute. Do you have any pain, in your head or elsewhere?"

"A bit, yes. I passed out, but I think I hit it when I landed. My neck aches a little as well, and my hip. Nothing feels especially bad, though."

"Do you feel sick or dizzy at all?"

"No."

From behind him, more movement, squeaks, and rustles as more spacesuited figures moved around John's body. I heard a crackle of radio.

"Can you tell me your name?"

"Bill—William Charles Cutter."

"Any blurring or doubling of vision?" He sat back at this last, eyes running over the rest of my body.

"No, I can see fine."

"Good." He let out a sigh, then he regained eye contact. "Can you remember what caused you to pass out?"

"Yes. It was looking at the blood pooling under John Cash's head. He's dead, isn't he?"

The man's eyes narrowed, and he frowned as he replied, "He is, yes. Do you know what happened to Officer Cash?"

"He was murdered by Jeff Slater - the bass player in my band - because he wanted Jeff to remove the song we wrote and recorded yesterday from YouTube. The song makes anyone who hears it have to tell the truth and kills people who refuse to by some kind of massive internal haemorrhage in the head, and it's already gotten over a hundred thousand views on YouTube.

"Jeff killed him then drove off with his laptop in his vintage green Mini, and he told me as he left he was going to try and boost the signal as big and wide as possible, and he took the hammer he used to kill John with him in his dressing gown. Which is blue and kind of grubby. The dressing gown, not the hammer. Also, he wasn't wearing a shirt."

The man lent over his shoulder, "Did you get that, Luke?"

I heard another voice say, "Yes, sir, I did, relaying to base," followed by a repetition of the description I'd given of Jeff. The man leaned over me again, looking at my eyes and then taking in my face. "Can you show me where you hit your head?"

I lifted my hand and pointed to the left side of my head, behind my ear. He felt gently with his gloved hands.

"Difficult to tell for sure, but it doesn't feel like a big lump."

"It isn't. I'm not concussed or crazy, though I am starting to wonder if this might not drive me there, sooner or later. I've been unable to tell a lie since we recorded the song at last night's band practice." The words felt like they barely belonged to me, my mouth and throat moving as if on wires.

The man in the Doc Brown suit stared at me.

"It's what happened at the school, okay? The dead boy and the teacher, they heard the song and then got asked questions they didn't want to answer, and they died. That's why you're wearing this suit, right? Because you're a quarantine paramedic and I might be contagious, right? That's why you're all walking around in those suits?"

He didn't respond directly. "You said your friend drives a green Mini. Do you happen to know his licence plate?"

No, I don't. It was an honestly held belief – I'd seen his car every band practice, but couldn't remember looking at the plate, let alone memorising it – but my mouth had other ideas.

"SK27 XED"

"Okay." He glanced over his shoulder and the officer who'd spoken before repeated the information into his radio. He looked at me some more. "If I step away for a moment, will you stay put until I get back?"

"I'd quite like to try and escape, but there's other officers in the room, I suspect we're surrounded, and I don't know for sure how bad my leg's hurt, so yeah, I'll stay lying down here until you get back. But, listen, you have to get the YouTube site taken down! Every second we waste, more people are getting affected and more people will die!" I could hear the desperation in my voice and hated how it made me sound weak, crazy.

He sat back on his haunches and looked at me, his

expression more frankly appraising than before. "If this is a delusion, it's a pretty unusual one. If it's an act, it's a very good one."

"You could test me, you know," I said, feeling panic threatening at the thought, but also desperate to make him believe me.

"How?"

I laughed. It wasn't a pleasant sound. "I can't lie. On pain of death. Like the kids say, 'Ask Me Anything!'" I felt panic in my chest as I said it and wished I could take it back.

He nodded. "That's certainly one way we could prove – potentially – that you *believe* you're unable to lie. But then I have my Hippocratic oath to consider. Would you like me to quiz you in that way?"

"Of course not! It's making me sweat just thinking about it!"

"Yes, I'd think so." He smiled, a tight little smile, there and gone. "First, do no harm. Also, legally, if you tell me something right now…" he waved his hands in a see-sawing gesture. "Who knows if it stands up?"

He stood and his knees clicked. "I'll go and talk to my colleagues outside. Won't be long. Please do lie still. I'm almost sure you're not seriously hurt, but any neck injury is potentially dangerous. I'll be back with a brace before we move you. Would you three come with me, please?"

I watched him move out of view and then heard him and his colleagues walk down the hallway to the front door.

At that moment, I remembered the phone in my pocket.

CHAPTER SEVENTEEN

I dug it out, then stared at the lock screen for a moment. After a near-miss concerning a borderline pornographic text from Sarah during our early courtship that had flashed up on my phone while it sat on my desk in class – I'd flipped the handset before any of the kids saw, but it was an incredibly close thing – I had push notifications turned off while the phone was locked and the device was still set to silent, though the row of icons along the top of the screen indicated that most of the ways people would normally try and reach me had been attempted.

I thought carefully about what to do next.

Phoning Jeff was the obvious choice, but I was worried that he might not answer; might, in fact, work out that he could dispose of the phone to avoid answering entirely. Text? Twitter DM? Facebook Messenger? Jeff had sworn off the big FB years ago, in the process of doing so, being the first person to introduce me to the phrase 'data mining' (though not its meaning, which eludes me to this day) but he'd begrudgingly created a Messenger account for band chat because it's all Steve would use.

Would it work? I tried to imagine receiving a question in written form, to see if I'd still feel compelled to respond, but I got no sense either way. My instinct was that it *would* work, but...

And it was the same problem as the phone call; he could just ditch his mobile, if he hadn't already, and not reply. Email? Surely, even if he ditched the phone, he'd have to keep the laptop in order to access the YouTube account.

That was when I worked out how to get it done.

I fired up the YouTube app and found our channel. The

song was there with last night's date and 'Untitled' as the track name. I thought about that, about the chances the song would ever get a name. I'd certainly never sing it again. And, yes, that did make me sad.

I was already signed in as myself, so I left a comment under the video: 'Where are you going, Jeff? And what are you going to do when you get there?'

I stared at the comment, wondering if he'd respond, if he was still driving. Trying to figure out what he could possibly be doing.

Forgetting that now the phone was unlocked, I'd start seeing push notifications again.

Forgetting that I'd set my text messaging to push notifications.

Remembering only when I saw the message from Sarah that read: 'What the FUCK is going on???'

Well, that answers that *question*, I thought, as I opened up the messaging app, compelled to reply.

CHAPTER EIGHTEEN

During my twenty minutes of unconsciousness, I now know that Jeff was driving and thinking furiously.

He knew the first order of business was getting rid of the car – I would be compelled to tell them about it, and anyway, they'd tie it to the address. He also assumed, correctly, they'd have an APB out on him based on my compulsion to tell them he'd murdered a policeman.

So, he'd need to change his appearance. Dump the car. Dump his phone, too – he wound down the window and threw it out, the Mini swerving slightly as the motion made him move the wheel of the car.

The laptop he'd have to risk – he knew he'd need it to keep the social media accounts plugging the video. Hopefully, they'd find it difficult to track if he kept moving.

He was also thinking about how best to spread the song far and wide. The sheer impossibility of what was happening gave him time; clearly, the authorities were treating this as some kind of infectious disease outbreak. The protocols for prevention would, therefore, do nothing at all to prevent the actual spread. At the same time, eventually, surely, someone would listen to what I was saying long enough to shut down the song on YouTube, even just as a precaution.

He had some ideas.

***

As Jeff pulled into the car park of the carvery in Peartree Bridge and left his beloved Mini behind forever, laptop tucked under one arm, leaving the keys in the ignition in the hopes that some enterprising tyke from the estate would steal it, I was replying to Sarah.

'I'm at Jeff's house. He's murdered a policeman that I broke the quarantine at the school with. I'm probably under arrest though that's not official yet. I was with a doctor, but he stepped out.'

I thought about adding kisses to the end of the message, then decided against it and hit send. Doing so caused a stab of pain, and I started typing out more information, filling in the blanks. I'd gotten as far as the details of what the song did and the death of Steven when the phone rang.

And because I was still typing frantically, I hit the answer button on the touch screen before I could stop myself.

"Are you taking the piss?" Her voice was just short of furious, but I could hear fear too, maybe even sadness. I sighed.

"I am not taking the piss."

There was a long silence then. I could hear Sarah breathing and could tell by her breath that she was pissed off.

"Sarah, I need you to understand something. Really hear me, okay? I know it sounds crazy, but... have you listened to the song yet?"

"You're sending me sick joke text messages about dead coppers and asking me that?"

"It wasn't a joke. And yes, I am, because—"

"Bill, I haven't listened to your fucking song, okay? I've been at work. Like I thought you were. Then I hear on the news there's been some kind of incident—"

"What did you hear?"

"An incident at your school, coppers and ambulances, I thought it had to be bullshit or you'd have gotten in touch."

"Love, I'm sorry, I would have done, but I've been so

rushed I didn't think to—"

"Look, it's not just the school. They're reporting mysterious deaths all over the country."

I felt my stomach clench. "How many?"

"I dunno, no one does, the reporting's a bit vague. At least a hundred."

A sob came out of me. I'd had no warning, couldn't stop it. I looked back over at John's body, still slumped in the corner of the room. I couldn't see his head, thankfully, but the immobile shape of him felt unbelievably solid; like the realest thing in the world – like the walls and the furniture and me and the rest was just... smoke.

"Bill..."

Don't ask don't ask don't ask...

"What the actual fuck is going on?"

Even as I started talking, my mind was racing, trying to find the most succinct way I could possibly tell it, get past the verbal diarrhoea and back to asking her questions. Because I'd realised a way that I – that *she* – could potentially stop the spread or, at least, slow it down.

"What's going on is the song we recorded last night causes anyone who hears it to tell the truth, the whole truth, and nothing but the truth, and if they try not to hard enough, they die because something ruptures massively in their heads and they bleed to death out of their faces. I've seen this happen with my own eyes. The deaths on the news are because of it, I'm sure. It's not a disease, it's the song. And Jeff uploaded it to YouTube last night and it's gone viral—"

I'd heard her sigh a couple of times as I was speaking, but it was here she interrupted with "It went viral? How?"

"I don't know – probably because it's a really good song and nobody has realised it's killing people. Anyway—"

"How many views?"

I remember blinking rapidly at this unexpected change of direction, but of course, my mouth was all, "Over a hundred K by half nine. Listen—"

"Holy shit! Nevermind the sub-Stephen King nonsense, you're a hit!"

I felt anger then. "Sarah, people are dying! I am not kidding around, okay? There's a dead policeman next to me. His name was John. I liked him, and Jeff murdered him, and now he's out there—"

"Jeff? Fucking Jeff?"

"Yes, fucking Jeff murdered the fucking officer."

"Bill, this isn't funny, okay? I don't know what this elaborate joke is about, but it's not funny."

I could hear her moving about as she spoke, and I heard the chime of our desktop starting up.

"Sarah, are you home?"

"Yes, I wasn't feeling well and the shop was dead, so they let me go home."

"What are you doing?"

"Why?"

"Because if you listen to that song, Sarah, you will never be able to tell another lie for the rest of your life, on pain of death, and I don't think you want to do that."

I could hear her breathing again. I closed my eyes.

"You really don't want me to listen to that song, do you?"

"No, I really don't."

"Why not? Is it about me?"

"No, it's not about you! It's about what the song will do to you—"

"Hang on. Are you telling me you've heard it? That you can't tell a lie?"

"Yes, that's right on both counts." My stomach sunk.

There was silence on the line. I heard footsteps in the hall.

CHAPTER NINETEEN

As I was teetering over the conversational abyss with Sarah, Jeff was knocking on the door of Derek Shelford.

It was an unpromising white door, the plastic at the bottom hanging off in a dangling strip. The house it was attached to wasn't much better; the end terrace of a row of decaying council homes, a motley collection of old vehicles stretching out along the cracked driveways.

Derek answered the door. Jeff had a second to take in the synchronicity of the moment – Derek's dressing gown was dirty black rather than dirty blue, his shorts khaki rather than denim, but the roached roll-up was perched in the corner of his mouth in a mirror image of Jeff. Jeff's eyes took in Derek's sunken chest and face, the paleness in his cheeks, the dark bags under eyes so bloodshot they were more red than white.

The baldness of his face and head stood in contrast to Jeff's shoulder-length mop, but, Jeff reflected, after three rounds of chemo, the fact that he was able to answer the door at all was a minor miracle.

Jeff gave Derek a moment to focus and was rewarded with one of his face-splitting grins, the roll-up miraculously staying glued to his lower lip. "Fuckin' hell, Jeff, what are you doing here at this ungodly hour?"

"I've found a way to save the world, Derek. I had to murder a policeman to do it though, so I am on the run. And now I need to steal the van, if you've still got it?"

Derek looked at Jeff, grin fading but not entirely gone. "I've still got the van, yeah, of course, you can borrow it if you need to—"

"Nah, mate," replied Jeff, cutting Derek off before he

could start with the inevitable and potentially conversation-and-friendship ending question. "I need to steal it, not borrow it. But before I do, I need some clothes and to shave my barnet. Can I come in?"

"Only if you promise to tell me how you're gonna save the world, you mentalist."

"It's a promise."

Derek opened the door. Jeff went inside.

***

Meanwhile, I was discovering the enormous utility for people with our condition of just boorishly pushing forward with the conversation, leaving no space for awkward questions. Especially when I could tell that I was soon to be joined by, at best, a paramedic, and at worst, a policeman.

"Sarah, I heard the computer start up; please, please, if you're going to YouTube, just at least turn off autoplay, okay? I don't know how much of the song you need to hear for it to affect you, but—"

"Okay, okay, fine, I will." I could hear clicking. It sounded angry, but I didn't care.

"Thank you. Are you at the song?"

"I think so. HOLY SHIT!"

"What, babe?"

"Five hundred thousand views! Fuck, it's ticking up as I look."

I felt my stomach lurch again, threatening nausea. Five hundred thousand. I pictured Mr Hopkins, his head fountaining blood. Mysterious deaths. All over the country. Shit, the world. Anywhere and anyone with access to YouTube.

"Is the laptop signed in to the band account or yours,

love?"

***

"Hey, Derek, mind if I fire up the laptop?"

"No, of course not, grab a pew, help yourself. Plug in over there. You checking emails?"

"No, I'm checking the new band song on YouTube. It's going viral."

"Wow, really? You going to be famous?"

"Yes, very, very famous." Jeff's eyes narrowed suddenly, his face flushed. "Oh, you little fucker…" his fingers started hammering at the laptop keyboard.

"So, can I get your autograph?"

Jeff slammed the laptop lid shut and turned to Derek. Derek's smile died as he caught Jeff's eyes. Jeff forced himself to smile, trying to plug into the genuine joy he was feeling, trying to ignore the anxiety and anger. He thought about how he and Derek had campaigned together, all those endless demos and marches and protests, even when Derek had gotten sick, his insistence to get out there, "Not dead yet" practically his fucking motto.

The van. Driving out to events and back, often the centrepiece of any sizeable street march.

The van, and how what was in the van had prevented several kettling attempts and more than one arrest.

"Derek, I will sign anything you like if you'll do me a favour and not ask me any questions until I've had a chance to get changed and shave. Deal?"

Derek returned a small, cautious smile and said, "Of course, mate."

***

Sarah's voice finally sounded a note of unease. "Okay,

that's weird."

"What?"

"I can see you asked a question, and the band account just replied."

"What did it say?"

My heart was pounding now. I didn't dare look up at the figure that had walked in and was now standing over me. The shadow felt like a threat and warning rolled into one; but I had to know.

"It says 'London. The rallies. And hopefully PMQs. And I meant it about the hammer.'"

The rallies. Climate Annihilation had estimated half a million people were headed for their demonstration at Trafalgar Square. Freedom From Europe was rallying at St James's Square – no one thought they'd get the same numbers, but after the last parliamentary vote, who knew? They were certainly motivated, and the media was bigging up the circus, even as the Met had been appealing, with increasingly ill-disguised desperation, for one or another organising group to blink. They hadn't, and the news had been calling it the biggest single day of policing in London in peacetime.

Hundreds of thousands of people. Maybe millions. In one place. If he could somehow broadcast or transmit the song...

And PMQs.

It was less clear to me how he'd get the song broadcast in the Commons, but...

"Is the laptop signed in as the band?"

"Yeah, it says 'The Fallen' at the top right for the account name."

"Thank fuck! Sarah, please go in and change the

password."

"Why do I need to do it? You've got YouTube on your phone."

"But it's not the band account and I don't have the sign in details. Jeff changed them. It's only still signed in on our PC because of that time he came over to ours after band and needed to upload the rehearsal track. If you change it now, it should shut Jeff out when he next tries to sign in."

"Bill, isn't this going to piss Jeff off? I don't want to be Yoko to your nonsense."

I tried hard not to let the frustration crawl into my voice. I failed. "The next time I see Jeff, if that happens, he'll try very hard to put a hammer between my eyes. Okay? People are dying, please…"

"Okay, okay, what password should I use?"

"Anything, something I won't know. Don't tell me."

"Fucking hell, Bill, all right, fine, done."

I let go of a breath I hadn't realised I was holding. "Thank you. Thank you, Sarah." I thought hard about the next step for about a second – which doesn't sound long, but it was enough for me to mourn the one-point-two thousand subscribers we'd built up through diligent plugging and relentless social media pushing over the last two and a half years. But what choice did I have?

"I need you to make the account private, then delete it entirely."

There was a long pause before Sarah replied. "I swear, if this is some kind of joke…"

"Sarah, please. Please. Every person who hears the song is a potential death. Please, help me try and fix this."

Another pause.

"You really can't tell me a lie? Because of the song?"

"I really can't, Sarah. Because of the song."

I could hear her breathing and I looked up at the figure standing over me.

He was tall, over six foot, broad-chested but slim. He was wearing the same white spacesuit deal as the paramedic had, but through the clear plastic of the helmet, I could see he had on a police uniform. He had dark hair, brown eyes, and just a hint of stubble along the jawline. His look was appraising, neutral bordering on vacant. It made me uneasy. I wondered why he was letting me carry on the conversation, but I didn't have time to think about it properly.

Instead, I opened my mouth to try and persuade Sarah to hurry up, and that's when she asked me, "What's the worst thing you've ever done?"

No. Not that.

I felt a rush of blood to my head. Stars behind my eyes. The stabbing pain ran deeper than before, feeling more like a ripping under the surface of my face, and I felt hot blood start to jet from my nose as I blurted, "I killed your brother!"

CHAPTER TWENTY

Jeff stepped back into Derek's living room. His head was now completely bald, including his eyebrows. He'd also appropriated a pair of Derek's tracksuit bottoms, the neck of a black T-shirt just visible under a zipped-up white hoodie.

"Wow, we're twins!" Derek managed a smile, but Jeff saw it was a poor effort.

"Now, Derek, where's the van?"

"It's in the lockup. We can walk over now if you want."

"No, that's okay. It's better for you if it looks like I nicked it. Makes it less likely you'll get dragged in." Jeff winced as he said this last as a jag of pain hit behind his eyes. "A bit less likely, anyway. But some shit might come your way. Sorry about that."

Derek frowned and Jeff felt sure he was going to start asking questions. He leant forward, placing his hands on the tabletop between them. "Derek, I swear to you, I think I've seen a way clear to fix everything. All that stuff we talked about, all those long drives? I think I've got the actual magic bullet. I know it's a big ask…"

That did the trick. Derek huff-laughed then reached behind him to the key hook, took off the ring that held the lockup and van keys, and slid it over the tabletop.

"Here you go, man."

"Thanks, dude!" Jeff grinned, feeling a surge of love for his old comrade powerful enough to hurt a little.

"No worries, man. Hey, you really think you're going to save the world?"

Jeff's grin grew wider. "Oh, yes, mate, I really think I might."

"How?"

Jeff's felt his eyes go out of focus as he spoke. "I'm going to make them all hear a song that'll make them all tell the truth. And if I can get it to enough people fast enough, I think things will take care of themselves."

While Jeff was talking, he'd reopened his laptop and started tapping away, inserting a flash drive into a USB port. As he finished talking, he snapped the laptop closed again and presented the drive to Derek with a flourish.

"What's this?"

"It's the song, Derek. The song that makes anyone who hears it tell the truth."

Derek looked down at the tiny rectangle of plastic and metal in his hands. He didn't look up as he started speaking. "Jeff, mate, I love you, but I'm struggling with this, I gotta be honest with you. It all sounds a bit far-fetched."

Jeff waited until Derek looked up at him again. "Mate, it sounds like the most mental thing ever. It sounds like fairy tale bullshit. I know all that. Just do me a favour, okay? Keep watching the news. The coverage from the demos. Or PMQs, if I get a wiggle on. Okay? See what you can see and make your own mind up. And if you like what you see and hear," he nodded at the flash drive, "remember, you've got the power, mate. This song can play forever if you want it to."

Derek nodded and finally did look up. "Godspeed, mate. Do some good."

Jeff's smile was sad but real. "Oh, I will. I'll do some bad, too. But mainly good. Thank you, Derek."

He took the keys, replacing them on the table with a

sizeable baggie of weed. He left without another word.

At some point, not long after Jeff left his house, Derek skinned up.

After a couple of tokes, he got out his mobile and made a call.

CHAPTER TWENTY ONE

I've heard people talk about a sense of relief when they finally unburden something, say out loud what they've carried for so long. A feeling of a weight lifting, of pressure removed; a lightness of being. Catholics swear by it.

I don't know if it's something broken in me or an effect of the song; maybe the fact that it's involuntary changes the act of confession, deprives it of meaning.

All I know is that in the moment after I had spoken the words I'd imagined I'd never say aloud, especially not to Sarah, it meant nothing. I felt no better.

In fact, I felt worse.

When Sarah spoke again, her voice had a quality I'd never heard. It was calm, but an *intense* calm, all deliberately even-toned and slightly clipped syllables. It made my heart hurt to hear.

"Bill, Sid died due to an allergic reaction. He had a severe nut allergy, and something on his camping trip triggered it and he died because he'd left the EpiPen in his car. That's it."

"No, that's not it. It was my fault—"

She tried to interrupt. "How can it possibly have been —"

But I was on a roll now, the words falling out of me like a pebbledash-shit the night after a dodgy takeaway. "It was my fault because of the cutlery I lent him. The camping cutlery, remember, that sat on a stand and fit in a carry case? I'd gotten them from Mum's caravan, they'd sat in the cupboard for years, in the case…"

I heard her breath catch, then even more calmly, she said, "But you cleaned them, you told me—"

"Yeah, I told you, but I lied. They *looked* clean and I told myself I just couldn't be fucked."

"But you know what a fucking demon your mum was for nuts! We used to joke about how her house was basically a death trap for Sid! He never went over there..." The calmness was starting to crack, fracture, and underneath, there was a sharpness that made me wince.

"It's worse than that. I told myself I just couldn't be bothered, but the truth is, I hoped it would happen."

She sobbed. I looked up at the officer standing over me. His face had turned from neutral to impassive, the corners of his mouth turned down, his eyes glittering and hard. I looked into those eyes as I continued talking.

"I couldn't stand Sid. I never could. Yeah, he had allergies, but he was a fucking martyr to them, and I hated it. I hated how he was always the total centre of attention whenever we were around your parents. When you told me about what growing up with him was like, even though you were kind about it—"

"Don't you fucking dare! Don't you dare put this on me! You fucking animal."

"I'm not! I'm not, it's on me, not you. I felt resentful on your behalf, all of his petty selfishness, the way your parents reacted to it, how he sucked up all their attention, all their affection. I saw it with my own eyes, that first Christmas—"

"That's not... I didn't..."

"You deserved the fucking world, Sarah, and they gave you scraps. All Sid's health problems, all his depression and misery, and you know what else—"

"I don't want, I don't... just stop..."

"He was a bad person, Sarah, he was. He was selfish, and mean, and I know he had it tough but it doesn't change the fact that he milked it mercilessly and he made everyone's life a fucking misery, and you were all better off without him."

"Fuck you! Fuck you!" She was shrieking now, loud enough that I saw the policeman flinch back. "I loved him, you fucking shit! We all loved him, and you took him away. And don't you dare, don't you dare—"

"I'm not, it's all me; it was selfish, I wanted you free from him because I thought you'd be happier in the long term," I tried so hard to stop there, but I felt an ache in my head and hastily added, "and I was right. You were. You are. You all are."

I felt tears on my own cheek then and realised my nose was running, snot mixing with the blood. Not thinking, I licked my lips. Salt and copper mingled on my tongue.

Her breathing was ragged now, almost feral. I opened my mouth, then closed it, realising with a surge of relief and guilt that I had nothing more to say.

Eventually, she replied, her voice barely a whisper. "I've deleted the account. I wish I could delete you, too, you fucker."

I closed my eyes, sending more tears rolling. I felt them drip off my chin. "Thank you."

"Fuck you. I hope you die a painful, lingering death, you vicious cunt. Don't ever fucking speak to me again."

The phone line went dead. I dropped the phone and curled into a ball. The tears felt like they were passing through me, making my whole body shake at their passage. Occasionally, the snot would build up in the back of my throat and I'd retch.

I had no sense of the passage of time, but I later found out I lay huddled in that spot for over thirty minutes. I was dimly aware of movement, more people tromping in and out, the officer's radio sending out bursts of conversation I couldn't make out.

As I came back to myself, I heard raised voices and a conversation – the words 'major incident' – and the sound of slamming doors and sirens blaring, then receding into the distance. It all felt distant, unimportant.

Then a hand gripped my shoulder. Painfully tight. I wiped my eyes with the back of my sleeve and looked up. The policeman was kneeling next to me, his expression that same stony neutrality I'd seen when I confessed to killing Sid. The memory of doing that forced tears back into my eyes and my vision doubled.

"Hey, cut that shit out, okay? We don't have time."

"What do you mean? Are you going to arrest me?"

"Very probably. But not just yet, no."

He leaned closer and I finally saw what the stoic face was hiding; anger, maybe even rage. His dark eyes glittered and his clean-shaven jaw was set, muscles in his cheek flexing. "I've heard the song, asshole. I know you're telling the truth. And I also know that means we've got to stop your mate."

Then he punched me in the nose. Hard.

It really hurt.

CHAPTER TWENTY TWO

I was only a few minutes into my foetal sobbing as Jeff, who had been heading for the M1, had a sudden idea, courtesy of the local radio. Following the headlines about a mysterious mobilisation of local police and ambulances to Lord Grey School (and about which Jeff had slightly more detailed information than the radio, due to the highly illegal digital police scanner that was sat under the driver side seat of the van), the final item was about the all-star charity football match taking place at the stadium. Local schools were taking part, and despite the midweek lunchtime kick-off, the event was sold out with queues already forming outside.

Jeff turned all the way around the next roundabout and then hit the gas.

It took him ten minutes to get to the stadium and the traffic was a crawl for the final grid road approach. It suited Jeff fine. He got the laptop out on the passenger seat and the MP3 of the song set up on the player, making sure it was on repeat. Then he plugged the lead from the dashboard into the headphone socket of the laptop and cranked the volume.

The song burst from the row of speakers mounted on the roof of Derek's van.

Jeff grinned, finger tapping the steering wheel along with the tune. It was a warm late summer day, and a lot of the cars in the jam with him had their windows down. He looked over at the stadium and the steady stream of people heading towards the queues gathered at each gate.

A couple of circuits of the car park should do it, then back on the A5 before anyone was the wiser.

Jeff started to whistle along with the song.

***

"You know where he's headed?"

"Yes. London. The rallies and probably the House of Commons. He said he wanted to hit PMQs." The blow to the face had made my eyes water, but there was no blood. I wondered if he'd had practice in punching someone in the nose just hard enough but decided it wouldn't be wise to ask.

The officer grinned, but it was entirely without mirth and it didn't do much for him.

"Well, fuck."

"Yeah."

"How, exactly, do you think he plans to do it, though? Rallies are fucking noisy places. And as to PMQs, I doubt anyone could smuggle in a broadcast stereo."

"I don't know. I mean, he's handy with tech, so maybe there's some kind of hack he can do. He's also a decent sound engineer, so maybe he can combine those somehow, get into the sound systems? There'll be PAs at the rallies, won't there? Sounds a bit James Bond, but I don't know how any of this shit works."

"Maybe he won't need that. Maybe the phone speaker will be loud enough for the song to carry from the visitors' gallery to the floor. Maybe you just need to hear it, not, like, understand what you're hearing."

"Yeah, maybe. Fucked if I know. Also, he's making this up as he goes along, he had no idea the song would do this, so…"

"Yeah. At least he's stumbling about as well. Still, what a total fuck-up." He'd been looking over the top of my head as he spoke, eyes flicking from side to side as he thought, but now they locked back on mine. "You know, I'm finding it quite hard not to beat the living shit out of you."

His voice was calm, but those brown eyes were burning with fury. I kept my mouth shut.

"I was listening to a local band mix on YouTube while I drove my daughter to school. She's six years old. My husband was supposed to be taking her, but he's struggling at the moment. So, I had to take a shift break, go home, pick her up, take her in, get back to the station." He took a couple of breaths. "It was sheer fluke that the song came on after I dropped her. If her or Rob had heard the song, I swear to God..." He closed his eyes, swallowed. The frown on his brow deepened, then slowly dissipated as he opened his eyes.

"Anyway. I know you didn't know this was going to happen, and that's fine, I suppose. I know it's not your fault, but it *is* your responsibility. And you and I are going to try and fix it, okay?"

"I'm fine with that, but how?"

"I don't know, but we know where he's going, so we can head up there. Maybe we'll figure out something more on the way."

"But what about the quarantine?"

The officer sighed. "It's fucking chaos out there, man. We're getting reports of mass casualties at the stadium and we were overstretched beforehand. They've gone over to local emergency protocols for mass unrest. The bad news is that means we've got maybe thirty minutes to get outside the city before it goes into lockdown. The good news is it means we'll be able to get out of here easily. I'm the only officer still at this scene. Help me out of this suit, would you?"

He turned around and I fumbled for the zipper. As I found it, I asked, "What happened at the stadium?"

The policeman started talking.

***

The event was scheduled to start properly at eleven, with an hour of pre-hype before the noon kick-off, but by 10:20, the good-natured queues had grown large enough that stadium management made the decision to open the gates early and let people find their seats.

As Jeff completed his slow circuits of the stadium, thousands of people heard some or most of the song as they filed in, scanning QR codes from printouts or apps.

At 10:30, with the stadium already one-third full, the PA system started piping out the usual mix of rock and pop songs. At 10:35, Jeff completed his second circuit and, noting the frowns he was starting to draw from the yellow-jacketed security people, he pulled out towards the A5 roundabout, leaving the song playing as he did so, passing the stream that was fast becoming a river of humanity flowing towards the stadium.

By 10:45, as Jeff was pulling onto the M1 (and already looking for a service station to pull into), the stadium was two-thirds towards its thirty-five thousand capacity, and Freddy Boyd, the Public Address match caller, had decided the crowd was big enough to make a little test broadcast, start the long warm-up to the noon kick-off. Freddy had been on-site since 7:30 and had already been up in his booth when Jeff was doing his rounds, and so had not been exposed to the song. He looked out through the glass at his beloved stadium (Winkleman may have done the legwork, fundraising, and the team acquisition, but none of that changed Freddy's heartfelt opinion that the stadium was *his*), and felt a surge of pride at the turnout, so strong it was almost painful.

He knew there'd be a big crowd from London today, given the nature of the event, but he also knew there'd be a big Dons contingent – and anyway, it was *his* stadium, *his* crowd, and he could see no reason not to start out as he always did on match day.

"Welcome to the MK Dons Stadium!"

A ragged cheer went up, especially from the season ticket area. Freddy could just make out the grins on the faces down there. They knew the score; this was all part of the match day ritual.

"You can do better than that! I said, welcome to the MK Dons Stadium!"

This time, most of the crowd cheered and a sea of arms went into the air. Freddy grinned.

"Now then..." He hesitated for just a moment, knowing it was a bit risky – not, after all, entirely a home crowd – before succumbing to well-worn habit and continuing, "Who thinks the Dons are going to go all the way this season?"

***

Michael Simmonds (always Michael, never Mike or Mickey), seven years old, was holding his father's hand when the question came over the PA. His old man was a die-hard True Believer when it came to the Dons, and when he'd found out his kid was going to be on the pitch as part of the event, he'd booked the day off work to make sure he was there to witness the triumphant moment.

"I'm so proud of you," Michael's dad had said to him – about a million times, Michael thought, since the announcement had been made months ago.

And now, here they were, and Michael, Cow Shed regular, knew this beloved call and response so well, he was on his feet yelling "YES!" at the top of his lungs, with all the surety of faith and lack of bitter experience his seven years conferred upon him before he realised his father's hand had gone slack.

He looked up.

Michael's dad's head was up, facing straight ahead, but

his shoulders had slumped, his arms hanging limply by his side. Michael saw his dad's face go pale, then turn red, then, as Michael stared on, jaw hanging open in a look that under other circumstances might have seemed comical, the red deepened to purple.

Michael was dimly aware that around him, people were making strange, choking noises, starting to scream. It seemed very far away. The only thing that felt really real, suddenly, was his father's increasingly odd-coloured face.

His dad's eyes opened, and he looked down at Michael. It was a moment Michael would remember for the rest of his life.

Then his father's eyes turned red before bursting. The sound was exactly like bubblegum popping. From the holes in his face where up until a second ago his father's eyes had been, blood jetted out, making twin arcs of red fluid that glittered in the late morning sun. Michael felt droplets land on his head, warm like summer rain, as the blood started to pour from his father's nose, ears, and mouth.

As his father fell to his knees, someone screamed – a terrible, high-pitched keening. Michael looked down into his father's sightless, ruined face, the blood soaking into the official Dons shirt his father had pulled on this morning before heading out to the stadium, and the screaming grew louder and higher.

His father fell forward, body slumping over the unoccupied seat in front, his forehead connecting with the concrete of the next terrace down, blood pooling there with a terrifying rapidity.

Michael stared for two minutes, not thinking of anything. Surrounded by choking yells, crying, puking noises, and that high-pitched keening.

Which, he eventually realised, was coming from him.

***

As we drove back to the station to pick up his civilian car, Officer Luke Anderson filled me in on what he knew about the developing situation at the stadium, which was, basically, carnage.

"They're estimating over a hundred casualties – most of them concentrated in the home supporters season ticket area, but some scattered elsewhere. Could your mate have hacked the PA system somehow, gotten the song played there?"

"I have no idea, maybe."

Luke's face was grim and sweaty – we'd dumped the spacesuit in Jeff's house before getting into the police car, and he'd run his hand through his hair as he talked, making it spike up. It gave him a wild, frazzled appearance which did me no good at all.

"Hopefully, we'll be able to work out more back at the station."

"Won't the stadium thing stop the London protests? Surely if they think it's a terror attack—"

"It's too fucking late. The marches have already started. If it was just Freedom From Europe, the local coppers might be able to get them to disperse, but CA could pull in a million, and they're already on the street. Nah, they'll just have to ride it out and hope for the best."

I had a lot more questions, then, but even a dullard like me was realising how dangerous *they* could get. However, I couldn't resist asking, "How come nobody has noticed you've been exposed yet?"

He glanced at me and the look was utterly withering. "I've got a husband," he said, as he turned back to the road. "The guys are civil enough, but I can count the number of actual friendships I've got in that station on your wife's dick. They're polite and professional, and they've been terrified to ask me anything personal since way before this morning's little event. It's not the first time I've been grateful for that. And we're a quasi-military institution. On a day like today, you don't get asked questions; you get given orders."

He glanced at me again. "There's one exception. One of the sergeants knows. She's a local music fan, too, we've been to a couple of gigs together." He raised a hand, "No, not your lot, and please, don't ask any questions about that or about the exact nature of how we worked out we'd been exposed, it's a long conversation and I need to be able to stop talking when we get to the station.

"Anyhow, I'm hoping she'll be there. She should be coordinating the emergency as long as she hasn't been caught out yet. I'll share with her what we know and, hopefully, she'll be able to find some clues as to what your friend," that last dripped with venom, "has been up to."

"Sounds good to me," I said. We fell into an uncomfortable silence that lasted until we made it to the station.

I spent quite a lot of the journey shaking, but no more tears came.

***

As we pulled into the police parking garage and made our way to Luke's civilian car (a Ford Galaxy in red), Luke shedding his uniform jacket and pulling on a plain black jumper, Jeff was parked in the van at the services, pounding the dashboard with frustration. The laptop was lying open on the passenger seat, connected to a charging pack that Jeff had paid an exorbitant amount for from the kiosk outside the gents' toilet.

The band's YouTube channel was gone.

Jeff checked the Twitter and Facebook feeds. The automatic messages he'd set up were still posting, but when he clicked on the links, he got 'sorry, something went wrong' YouTube errors. The comments on the Facebook wall for the video were already turning grumpy.

"That little shit!" he said aloud, staring without seeing at the page.

Okay, well, okay. He could re-upload the video directly to Facebook. The viewing figures would be for shit because Facebook buried posts from pages that were not boosted financially, but it would at least put it back out there, give him something to point people at. A pinned Tweet with the video direct there, too?

Jeff opened a row of tabs and started the upload process for Twitter and Facebook. The Wi-Fi from the services' KFC was woeful, but what choice did he have? While he waited for the upload bars to crawl across, he opened a fresh notepad page and began typing the messages to accompany the new posts.

He also opened the glove compartment to make sure the hammer was there. Muttering "Fucker" under his breath, he went back to typing.

CHAPTER TWENTY THREE

Luke and I were just pulling onto the M1 when his phone rang. He looked at the name, Lena, grunted, and hit the speakerphone button.

"Hey, Luke?" The woman's voice had a European accent and an urgent tone.

"Speaking. I have William Cutter here, too. He's the man who sung the song that's so perfectly fucked up our mornings."

I cringed back in my seat.

"You're sure you can trust him?"

He looked at me. "He confessed to murdering his wife's brother in front of me. The song has clearly had the same effect on him as the rest of us, and he's told me he didn't know it was going to do this, so there we are."

I felt a surge of blood rushing into my head, heart hammering at the memory, stomach-churning, the guilt a solid, painful thing. Not just guilt, either; not even mainly guilt. Shame. Shame at the fact of what I'd done being out in the world, known outside of my own head. The guilt was something I'd carried for years; a known quantity. The shame was new, and it flooded my system with a surge of prickly heat. I wondered if I was going to faint again.

"Fair enough. Listen, I've got something, but I'm not sure it's your guy. Before the incident at the stadium, a van with roof-mounted speakers was seen driving round, playing a single song on repeat. Security assumed it was a punter at first, then maybe someone trying a publicity stunt of some kind. They were considering pulling it after the second circuit but then it drove off."

"Fuck, that must have been him!"

Luke waved me to silence, his face intense, eyes locked on the road. "Give me a description?"

"White, male, thirties, bald."

"Eye colour?"

"Nope. But we got the plates."

"Well, fucking hell, don't leave us in suspenders, Sarge!"

She laughed. "One Derek Shelford of Fishermead, Milton Keynes."

Luke looked over at me. I shook my head. "I take it he's getting a visit?"

"From half the armed coppers in the county, yeah. The press is starting to call the stadium a possible terror attack. Thank fuck all I've had to do is give and take orders so far. I'm one question away from a suspension."

Luke laughed. "If we don't stop this geezer, Sarge, that's going to be all of us soon enough. Do we have anything on this Shelford bloke?"

"Couple of arrests for protesting, civil disobedience stuff. Stop the War, Greenhouse Holocaust – so, he's old school – but nothing from the last five years."

"How soon until the team gets there?"

"Five minutes."

"Fine. Call me back when you know more. And text me the plate number for the van?"

"Will do. Hopefully, they'll nab the nutter at this guy's house."

"That'd be nice, but my gut says they won't."

"Yeah, mine either," said Lena and ended the call.

Thirty seconds later, a licence plate number flashed up on the text alert.

"What do you think?" Luke glanced at me quickly before turning his attention back to the road. Traffic was getting heavy, bunched up by the roadworks and the accompanying fifty-mile-per-hour limit.

"He said he was heading for London. I think it was him in the van, and I think that van is somewhere on the road ahead. He could have taken a less direct route, but if he's serious about PMQs, and he must be, then time's going to be tight, and even with all this shit," I gestured at the forest of cones we were passing, "this is the most direct route in."

Luke sighed. "Yeah, that's what I think, too. Fuck it, I wish I had the blues to run." He edged the speed up to fifty-five and moved over to the centre lane.

***

Jeff glanced down at the clock on his laptop as he frantically jabbed at the keys. "Fuck!" 11:00. Already really pushing it for PMQs. The rallies would be nice, he could certainly catch a lot of people with the van speakers, but he desperately wanted to get to the politicians and press, that would really get the ball rolling. Especially with the live TV and webcasts. He'd reach millions, and once the footage was out...

He looked back at what he'd been doing. The new YouTube channel was up and running with the video renamed 'THE SONG THEY TRIED TO BAN!!!' (might as well lean into the situation, he reflected, when he hit on the idea), and he'd put links in the replies to the Facebook post and Tweet where the original YT link had been. Whoever had shut down the YouTube account either didn't have the other platform sign-ins or had forgotten about them. Good. Still, looking at the play count under the new upload crawling towards the one hundred mark hurt his heart.

"Fuck it," he said to himself as he turned the key in the ignition. Let him get to the House of Commons. If he could just do that, by the evening, the song would be global. Too big to stop.

The police scanner had been crackling away to itself, full of the activity around the stadium and quarantine preparation, but just as he was engaging first gear, he heard Derek's name and address.

"Fuck!" he said, his foot slipping off the gas, causing the engine to stall. The burgundy Prius that was reversing into the slot next to him stopped its manoeuvre suddenly, and he raised a hand in distracted apology to the harried-looking woman – blonde, middle-aged, and to Jeff's way of thinking, rather too much makeup, especially around the eyes – who was sat behind the wheel.

As she returned to her cautious parking, he turned up the volume on the scanner, listening with mounting dread as what sounded like half of Thames Valley Police's armed response units closed in on his friend's house.

Fuck, thought Jeff.

If they had Derek, they either had or were about to have the van. Cameras all over the M1. Could they track it based on the plates? Jeff didn't know for sure, but his bet was yes.

Fuck.

He caught his own eye in the rear-view mirror of the car. His bald face looked pale and haunted; like he'd somehow contracted Derek's cancer by appropriating his look. Gritting his teeth, he looked in the passenger side mirror. He saw the woman rummaging in her handbag, eventually pulling out a huge bunch of keys with a black plastic fob. He saw her clutch that in her left hand before opening the car door and stepping out.

Jeff made a decision. He switched sides, clambering over the gear stick to sit in the passenger side.

As the woman walked past, he threw the door open as hard as he could. The rigid side mirror hit her high on the temple and she was already slipping from her feet as he jumped down from the van and grabbed her.

He moved fast. It took him less than forty-five seconds to manhandle her into the boot of her own car.

It was on the way back to the front of the car that he spotted the child seat through the passenger side window.

The baby in it stared at him.

CHAPTER TWENTY FOUR

Luke and I had just passed Toddington services when the phone rang. Lena. Luke answered it. "You're on speaker with me and Bill."

Lena started talking rapidly. "We're in Derek's flat but he's gone. So's his van. There's a load of hair in the bathroom though, so it looks like our guy may have shaved his head. In which case, that was him at the stadium. There was already an APB out on the van, so we're just waiting to hear back from traffic. It's fucking chaos down here with the stadium response or we'd probably have gotten something back by now. Any joy on your end?"

"No," said Luke, and I could see the muscles in his jaw clenching and unclenching, almost like a pulse. I wondered if he knew he was doing it but decided not to ask. "We're stuck in the fifty zone still. Any idea how much more of this shit we've gotta get through? I'm worried if he had a head start that he's getting further away."

"The roadworks run to Junction 9. But if he's anywhere on the M1, the cameras will definitely get him; they're clocking all the plates on the road for the average speed traps... hang on a sec." There was a muffled sound on the other end of the phone. I opened my mouth to speak, but Luke made a shush noise, actually putting his finger to his lips, furious.

I shushed.

There was muffled conversation, a low male voice, and tones that I recognised as Lena's. This went on for a couple of minutes, then there were footsteps. Around us, the traffic moved on, fifty miles an hour feeling like a crawl, cars moving over and taking Junction 11A. Luke's jaw was still going, the bulging muscles moving faster. The urge to say something, ask something, grew and grew, but I held it in. I remember thinking that those of us who had been affected would need to get used to silences, uncomfortable or otherwise.

There was more rustling on the line and Lena's voice came back strong. "Sorry, it's fucking nuts down here. Listen, we've found the van."

Luke punched the dashboard, a quick, hard jab. "Where?"

"Toddington services."

"Fuck! We just went past Junction 11A. Fuck!"

"There's a footbridge that connects the north and southbound services if you can get over—"

"Got it." Luke jabbed a finger at the phone, turning it off, then signalled left, pulling across to the slow lane. "You're going to want to hang onto something."

"Why?" I asked, the question pure reflex.

Luke grinned, but it looked pained and unhappy. "Because I'm about to take us off at Junction 11A via the on-ramp, and there's a non-trivial chance we'll end up in a head-on collision. I'm a bloody good driver, but it's a stupidly dangerous thing to do with many elements out of our control. Any other dumbfuck questions?"

Of course, I did have one. "Do we have to?"

His eyes darted in my direction for a split second before turning back to the road. "No. But we're fucking going to. Hang on."

***

The Prius was an automatic – and a hybrid, which Jeff wasn't sure he understood but didn't seem to make any difference to the driving experience – and it had been more than a decade since he'd driven without gears. He found his hand kept falling to the drive stick when he was slowing or accelerating, and more than once his right foot had moved over for a clutch pedal that wasn't there, tapping the brake instead. Thank fuck for the roadworks, he'd thought – if he'd made some of those sudden decelerations at speed with someone on his arse, he could have already gotten into an accident.

Jeff wiped sweat from his forehead. The heating was on full blast and he didn't know how to turn it down. He'd gotten the woman into the boot easily enough, the disorientation of the blow to the head had done most of the work and the implied threat of the hammer the rest, but every second he'd spent transferring the police scanner, child seat, and laptop between vehicles, he'd felt fear clawing at his insides, his skin crawling like a hundred eyes were fixed on him. He'd kept his head down, not looking around. Trying to move with confidence, knowing the easiest way to draw attention was to look nervous; still, it had been a relief to get behind the wheel of the car and shut the door. There had been a moment of panic when he'd been able to find neither the ignition slot nor the key on the locking device, but he'd quickly spotted the 'start' button on the dashboard and, after a few seconds fucking about, realised he needed the brake pedal depressed before the engine would start.

He'd pulled out carefully, enjoying the smooth running of the car after the jostling suspension of the van, and tried not to think about the look on the woman's face as he'd slammed the car boot door down.

He kept seeing it, though, as he navigated the fifty-mile-an-hour traffic and cursed his constant attempts to change gear. He'd turned the scanner off before transferring it into the car, and he'd been in such a hurry to get moving he was ten minutes back into his journey, just passing under an overpass, when he remembered.

He reached over with one hand, eyes flicking between the on switch for the black box that sat on the passenger seat and the road ahead, the sweat really rolling off him now, the stress of the situation adding to the heat from the air vents. His finger was slippery enough and the angle just poor enough that his finger slipped off on his first attempt.

As his car cleared the bridge, he looked back at what he was doing and this time, the scanner burst into life as the switch snapped into place.

As he looked back at the road, two pieces of information collided in his brain.

The first came from his ears, which were telling him that the police had located his van at Toddington services and were sending units and a forensics team to that location.

The second came from his eyes, as a red Ford Galaxy, about a hundred feet and three vehicles in front of his, veered sharply to the left, tyres squealing, and accelerated up the on-ramp, directly into the merging traffic.

***

Luke turned the wheel and tapped the brakes, slamming the accelerator to initiate a skid that would take us onto the on-ramp. My stomach lurched and my arm slammed up against the roof to steady myself. The traffic through the window was a blur, a streak of colours. Then the grill of the eighteen-wheeler suddenly filled the windscreen, horn bellowing like a ship in fog.

I was certain it would be the last thing I ever saw – I remember thinking *we're going to die,* and the feeling attached to the thought was not fear but misery, a rancid self-pity that made me feel dirty.

Luke let out a yell – fear, elation, I couldn't tell you, but something raw, elemental – and wrenched the steering wheel, slamming his foot down on the gas. The engine roared, howled, I felt the car shimmy, had time to think, clearly, *This is it,* then I felt the tyres bite as I was pushed to the left, leaning out into the centre of the car as we slid sideways, missing the front of the lorry by inches.

Luke's side of the car struck the wall. The blow slammed me back to the right, my head bouncing off the window. Even through the stab of pain, the noise from Luke this time was unmistakable; he laughed as he steered us off the wall, still accelerating in a low gear, the engine sounding like some great beast in pain, the smell of rubber and burning oil filling the car.

We stayed over on the far right of the feeder lane, the needle pushing forty as Luke finally changed gear, the steady stream of oncoming cars all lurching away as they saw us, horns blaring, faces flushed with anger and fear. Luke kept laughing, loud enough to hear over the engine as we hit the top of the slip road.

The roundabout was light controlled and sheer blind luck had changed it to red just before we hit the top of the ramp. We fishtailed in behind a National Express coach, and Luke finally hit the brakes. Behind us, I could hear horns, screeching tyres, and the sound of impacts and breaking glass.

We hadn't died. But that rancid feeling remained.

***

For Jeff, time had seemed to slow as our car performed the turn onto the on-ramp. He saw my face, pale and frightened, and Luke, grimacing in fury or joy. His eyes moved from there to the car in front of him. The brake lights shone at him, and the distance was closing fast. He realised he had exactly this moment in which to decide how to react and to commit to that course of action.

He accelerated.

He swerved right as he did so, pushing his car in between the left and middle lanes, passing between the slowing traffic. He kept his foot down, feeling the engine kick in, propelling the car forward.

Something – something huge – moved in the left of his peripheral vision. He heard the bellow of an air horn, the sound of tyres in pain, and he concentrated on threading the gap in front of him. The cars were swerving, but in each case away from him, peeling off to the left and right. The shape continued to close, but Jeff didn't look back, urging the car forward, needle pushing past seventy into eighty, his teeth grinding together.

The shadow of the lorry passed over Jeff's rear-view mirror, impossibly close. There were a series of loud crunches from behind him. Jeff chanced a split-second glance at the mirror and saw the eighteen-wheeler across all three lanes, cab resting on the central reservation, bonnet crushed and bellowing dirty steam.

That might actually make life easier, thought Jeff. Then he turned his concentration back to the road ahead. Still accelerating. Looking for the next junction.

CHAPTER TWENTY FIVE

We drove back to the northbound services in silence. I stole a couple of glances at Luke, but what I saw didn't invite conversation; his face was flushed, his grin fixed and painful looking. I was also acutely aware that I didn't feel safe speaking, full stop. Any opening gambit would almost have to be in the form of a question, and questions had become dangerous; even lethal.

So, I sat in silence, fear churning my stomach, hands and arms trembling from reaction until we pulled into the services.

As soon as we parked up, Luke was out of the car and running for the overpass. I tried to keep up, but he had maybe five years on me, and even if he hadn't, he was in far better physical shape. Also, I kept seeing the grill of the lorry cab, seeming to fill my entire field of vision, bigger than the world, my mind superimposing the sideways impact I'd felt as the car hit the wall with what would have happened if we'd gone headlong into that thing.

My mouth was already dry (when had I last taken a sip of anything?), and all at once, that dryness felt painful, suffocating.

I dropped to my knees halfway across the bridge and started retching. Most of what came up was an acidic fluid and the aftertaste was bitter. I kept my eyes shut for a few moments as I gulped down air and willed my stomach to settle.

When I opened my eyes, my breath caught in my throat.

The entire southbound lane was stationary. The cars were bumper to bumper, stretching back past the entrance to the services. As I stood up slowly, I watched the tail get added to as more and more vehicles came to a halt, turning the entire road into a parking lot.

We did that, I thought, and felt light-headed. I resumed crossing the bridge on legs that were not quite steady.

***

I had to stop again once I'd gotten across the bridge, legs and lungs aching, so I used the elevated position to scan the car park of the services.

I was looking for Luke, but I spotted the van.

It was in a bay not far from the car park entrance, backing onto a scrub line of bushes. The bays on either side were empty, the distance from the actual services making it an unattractive spot, I supposed.

I half-limped down the stairs, my leg muscles loudly protesting about my second attempted sprint in a day, and walked over to the van. Luke was there, grin gone, face flushed and angry.

"Your mate is a bit of a cunt," he said, gesturing at the van.

"I know that," I said, then following Luke's pointed arm, stopped talking.

The baby in the baby seat that was sat in the passenger side of the van stared at me.

Jeff, what are you doing? Looking into that empty, innocent face, my eyes stung with tears.

I turned back to Luke, but he already had his mobile phone to his ear, other hand held up in a warning gesture; *shush.*

I shushed.

A few seconds ticked by, then he started talking.

"Lena, can you talk? Okay, we've found the van, but the

prick has switched vehicles... I don't know, but it had a child seat... Because he left the baby in the seat in his van... Yes, yes he is."

He shifted his feet as Lena spoke, eyes darting between me and the baby in the van.

"Well, someone's going to need to get down here, pick up this baby. No, no obvious identifying features – it's a fucking baby." Pause. "Oh, that's fucking perfect." Pause. "I had to, it was the only way to get here, though, of course, I've always wanted to try something like that. He may have still been here." Pause. "Good idea, call me back."

Luke looked at me, brow knotted, jaw out, shoulders hunched. "She's just trying to figure out what time the van made it into the services. If we're lucky, maybe he got caught up in that shit," Luke waved a hand at the line of stationary vehicles taking up the southbound lanes.

"I don't feel remotely lucky," I said.

"Nor do I," said Luke.

We stood in silence until the phone rang.

***

Jeff still hadn't figured out how to turn the heating down and was wondering if both the woman in the trunk and the child he'd left in his van could possibly be lizards or something. He had, however, worked out how to get the windows down, and the late summer breeze was counteracting the worst of the hot air belching from the fans, spreading a welcome chill across his sweat-coated head and face.

The scanner told him they'd located the van at the services, but also that there weren't any officers on the scene – and furthermore, thanks to the articulated lorry that had come within inches of flattening Jeff and the Prius he rode in on now laying across the entire southbound artery, getting there was going to take a minute. Especially as they were massively overstretched with the 'terrorist incident' at the stadium.

Jeff looked at the time on the dashboard. 11:17. His eyes flicked back up to the road ahead. So far, the traffic was still flowing, still moving at bloody fifty miles an hour, but at least still moving. Regardless, Jeff knew he had to get off the motorway. The same cameras that picked up the van would find this car eventually... *if* the pigs managed to figure out he'd stolen it. Were there cameras in the car park? He'd not thought to look, too busy moving on impulse.

He shrugged. Too late to worry about it now.

He sighed with relief as Junction 11 came into view and he moved over into the left-hand lane. Luton. There'd be cameras in the town centre, probably, but that was okay, he thought; he knew the town well enough between the gigs they'd played there and the odd airport protest with Derek. Navigating to London from there without using the motorway might have been more of a challenge, had he not lucked into this particular vehicle. He looked back at the dashboard on the Prius and the display screen with the NAV button next to it.

He smiled.

CHAPTER TWENTY SIX

It was a long three minutes before Lena called back, and I was finding the silence between Luke and I oppressive enough that I sighed with relief as the ringtone started and he answered.

"It's me." Pause. He took the handset away from his ear and looked at the display, then placed it back. "You're sure? 10:57?" Pause. "Fuck, that's close." He made eye contact with me. "So, he could well be caught in the jam?"

Sure.

"No."

Luke stared at me, a look of surprise on his face so total that I had to repress a terrible urge to laugh. He lowered the phone from his ear and I could vaguely hear a woman's voice coming from the tinny speaker.

"No? He's not in the jam?"

I don't know.

"No, he isn't."

"What the fuck, Bill?"

"I don't know."

"How do you know he isn't in the jam?"

I don't, I...

"I saw him."

Luke scowled and I saw the muscles move under his shirt as he ended the call, hard enough to make the phone case creak.

I kept talking. "I saw him, but I didn't know I'd seen him, it was when you pulled the skid to take us off the motorway, he was behind the wheel of a dark red Prius, I saw it but I didn't remember it, I *don't* remember it, but I know it's true because you asked..." The not-memory sparked another connection, and I yelled "The licence plate! It's like Jeff's Mini, when the guy asked me for the plate, I knew I didn't know it, but then I did, I just answered."

Luke's frown unknotted. "What..." he stopped again. I could see he was struggling, trying to make sense of it, and I thought of a way to help him along.

"Tell me what you were doing this exact time and day when you were three years old."

"I was laying across my father's stomach, watching the Muppet show while he talked on the phone. He was talking about his work, but I didn't understand the words, I was just enjoying the rumble of his voice on my cheek as I watched Gonzo on a motorbike." Luke turned pale as he spoke, his eyes wide.

"Do you remember any of that?" I asked.

"No! No, but..."

"But you do. Some part of you does, and thanks to the song, you *can* remember it. Some part of you can, anyway."

Luke exhaled. "Fucking hell."

"Yeah," I said.

We held eye contact. Then Luke said, "What was the number plate on Jeff's Prius?"

***

Jeff took the opportunity of his first red light in the town of Luton to turn his attention to the heating system, and after a few seconds of trying switches, he found the main temperature control and turned the air to cool.

The police scanner crackled away. They hadn't yet made it to the van, thanks to the colossal tailback that was still growing. The issue was exacerbated by the fact that most of the services were engaged in either the stadium aftermath or the wider Milton Keynes quarantine effort.

That was good, Jeff reflected, but still, it was probably best that he stayed off the motorways. He looked at the clock again. 11:23. Jeff thought about Luton to Westminster in forty-five minutes without motorways, and with a deep, shuddering sigh, let go of the idea of hitting PMQs.

That left the rallies.

He thought about the two groups. Freedom From Europe were, in Jeff's opinion, proto-fascist scum, and the thought of broadcasting the song out over their PA, then watching the fountain of white, pinhead brain haemorrhages that would ensue as soon as they tried to shout one of their lying slogans filled Jeff with a wave of pleasure so powerful it was almost sexual.

On the other hand, their protest was likely to be relatively small – the last 'grand rally' had attracted barely ten thousand protesters and the violent clashes with the police that marred the end of the demonstration had put a lot of normies off the movement, if the internet chatter was to be believed.

Climate Annihilation might pull a million.

And he *knew* them. At least some of them. He thought about trying to get to the PA at the FFE stage. He supposed he had the look now – white, male, skinhead – but they were such a paranoid bunch, they'd probably have Football Lads or similar running 'security'. Climate Annihilation, on the other hand...

He pressed the NAV button on the right of the screen built into the Prius dashboard. The touchscreen was sluggish, and his attention was divided between the screen and the slow-moving town centre traffic, but he finally got a route programmed to Trafalgar Square, avoiding motorways. Sixty-five minutes, according to the satnav. Jeff thought he'd be lucky to get there before one. In fact, with the march causing road closures, he wouldn't be getting all the way there at all in the Prius.

As he followed the first instructions of the satnav for his chosen route, he heard the first mention from the police scanner of something called the Finite protocol.

***

Luke rang Lena back as we jogged across the bridge, back towards the car, and gave her the licence plate the song had dragged up from my mind. I tried to hear the conversation over my own heavy breathing, with limited success.

As we climbed back into the car, Luke hung up the phone, mounted it in the dashboard clip, and started talking to me.

"Lena will call back when traffic picks up the plates. If he sticks with the M1, we'll find him. In the meantime, we're going to head south, avoiding that shit show, of course." He jabbed a thumb at the stationary traffic glinting in the bright autumnal sun, then started the engine, pulling us smoothly out of the car park.

"Okay, but he's not going to be on the motorway," I said, surprised at the words. *And I know this how?*

Luke glanced at me quickly before returning his eyes to the road. "And you know this how?"

I don't...

"He saw us. Saw me. He knew it was me, I know from how his shoulder moved, brow wrinkled. He saw me, he knows I'm after him. Knows you're with me. He won't know you're a cop but he's paranoid enough to suspect it. So, he'll know we know the car, so he'll stay off the motorway to avoid the cameras."

Luke smiled, but it was close to a sneer. "Fucking Sherlock over here."

"It's not funny, this is scaring the shit out of me."

"Yeah? Well, fuck you, mate. If it wasn't for you, this wouldn't be happening at all, so having the shits put up you is the very least you deserve."

I looked over at Luke, surprised by the roughness in his voice, and saw he was close to tears; throat working, blinking too fast, eyes narrowed. The question bubbled up – *Are you okay?* – and I drew breath to ask it when the phone rang.

Luke jabbed the pickup button. "Lena. You're on speaker with Bill the fuckhead."

"Bill the fuckhead's mate got off at Luton. He's moving through the city centre and he's still heading south."

Luke glanced at me quickly before speaking "He's staying off the motorways to avoid the cameras. Will you still be able to track him?"

"For a bit, but not much longer. They're moving to the Finite protocol."

"Fuck!" Luke's knuckles on the steering wheel turned white. "When?"

"Not sure. Soon."

"But the rallies in London!"

"Yeah, it's going to be fucking bedlam."

"Okay, please track him as long as you can, let us know if he changes course."

"I will."

Luke turned the phone off. "You don't want to know," he said through clenched teeth.

He was right. I didn't want to know.

But I *had* to.

"What is the Finite protocol?"

CHAPTER TWENTY SEVEN

Luke's voice was a flat monotone as he drove. "It's a disaster protocol. It's activated when there's a national-scale threat of some kind – chemical, biochemical, nuclear. It's a way to mass coordinate emergency services under centralised army command. The name is also the function; it's a way to ensure the finite resources of the services are rationally allocated in the event that something is happening either big enough or in enough places at once that we can't cope with it all." He swallowed, eyes fixed on the road ahead. "It's the national emergency services management programme for the end of the UK. And your song has triggered it."

I thought about the five hundred thousand views on the YouTube video and my stomach swirled uncomfortably.

I spoke to distract myself. "So why are you worried about the protests?"

"Because, genius, one of the first things that happens under Finite is a martial law declaration."

"Oh. Oh, shit."

"Oh, as you so rightly point out, shit."

The phone rang. Luke answered it. "Speaker. Me and dickhead."

"I'm getting moved as part of Finite prep, so I can't help anymore with the tracking. Last I saw, he's still heading London-bound from Luton." She gave us a road name. "Sorry."

"Not your fault. Hopefully talk soon."

"Probably not, but you never know." This time, she

ended the call.

Luke glanced at me. "I don't know Luton too well. Can you put the road name into the satnav for me?"

"Almost certainly," I said, glad of the distraction. It took me a couple of minutes, as turning the wheel to select the letters for inputting was not something I was used to, but I got it done.

I looked up at Luke, planning to ask him what we were going to do when we got to the road in question – how we were going to keep tracking Jeff – but I saw the tears running down his cheeks, so instead, I asked softly, "What's wrong, Luke?"

He laughed – a sad, choked sound. "What's wrong, my little dickheaded friend, is my life its totally, utterly, irreversibly fucked, that's what. My *job* is totally fucked. Can't be a copper if you can't lie. First time a superior officer asks me a stupid question or a suspect asks me a smart one, I am totally done. Only thing I was ever good at, only job I ever wanted. I always hated bullies, and this was my way of stopping them, helping people, and ten years in, that's me done, see you later.

"My marriage is fucked, too. I don't love my husband anymore. Haven't for years. He's got mental health issues, anxiety, panic attacks, it's gotten worse and worse. He's too fucking sensitive – politics, global warming, all that shit filling his head. He's been in and out of his job. He's off sick home today, that's why I had to take Charlie to school..." He swiped away the snot that was almost on his lip with the back of his hand as he continued talking, "... because my man, Rob, he can't hack it anymore, can't hack being in this world, really, and I tell him it's okay, and I tell him he'll get better, but it isn't and he won't, and I don't love him anymore."

Luke's hands gripped the steering wheel tight, eyes streaming but fixed on the road ahead. "He had a panic attack with my daughter in the car, you fucking believe that? Thought he was having a heart attack. She was four. Sat in the car thinking Daddy Rob's dying, and it's all just in his head, you know? Man, fuck him and his weak bullshit, endangering my little girl. I can't stand him.

"But she needs him, and I need her, so I tell him I love him and I fuck him when I have to, and I go to work and do what I can to make the world less shit and I could have held on like that, at least until she got older, I could have bullshitted it was okay, but not now. Not thanks to you and your fuckhead mates. Now, the next time Rob looks me in the eye and tells me he loves me – and he does, you know, that's the real fucker – I won't have shit to say back."

Luke swallowed, and a shuddering sigh ran through him. "Add in the fact that the next time Charlie plays the why game with me, she's going to find out Santa's not real, and yeah, that's my entire life comprehensively fucked, mate, so that's what's wrong."

We drove on in silence. I thought about Sarah, the cold hate in her voice when the call finished, probably the last time I'd hear her voice. The look in Kelly's eyes as she held Tommy, sobbing his guts out over the friend he'd accidentally killed.

Then I thought about the five hundred thousand views and Jeff, somewhere up ahead, that laptop containing a poison pill that was really a bomb; a device whose capacity for destruction was almost unimaginable.

The guilt I'd carried for Sid, I'd earned; I deserved it, and maybe I deserved to lose the things I'd lost today because of what I'd done. But the song had been an accident; I was more sure of that than almost anything else. We hadn't been trying to change the world, even in the dumb figurative way musicians and songwriters pretend they will when they pen some anthem they imagine will change perspectives and reprogramme minds. We just wanted to have some fun and make people feel good. That was all.

Trying to put it right, limit the damage; that wouldn't clear the slate, nothing could. I understood that clearly. But it would make a difference, so it was worth trying.

If I'd known what awaited us in London, there's a good chance I'd have thrown myself out of the car right there.

Instead, I thought back to the moment Luke spun the wheel to take us off the motorway; that grin-grimace on his face.

It was a stupid question. A *dangerous* question. But he was driving the car. I had to know.

"Luke, are you suicidal?"

His reply was a flat monotone, the tears already starting to dry on his cheek. "Not exactly, but I don't give a shit if I live or die anymore. I want to stop your mate. By killing him, ideally. I wouldn't mind killing you, either, but you're helping, so I can't really bring myself to.

"After that, though, I don't give a shit what happens to me because I'm not me anymore; I'm fucking Rain Man. Have to spend the rest of my life wearing fucking ear plugs to avoid spilling my guts to any fucker who thinks to ask me anything."

I couldn't think of anything to say and I couldn't bear looking at his face; he was utterly stricken. I looked at the satnav instead.

Ten minutes to destination.

What the fuck were we supposed to do then?

***

Jeff almost missed the lights change – a combination of banging from the boot, which had started up shortly after they hit town (he thought because the woman in the boot had realised they were in a populated area), and the increasingly odd chatter from the scanner taking his mind away from the road. He made the left-hand turn, raising a hand in apology to the car behind.

"Turn right in two hundred yards."

"...Be advised, Finite protocols have been initiated, all mobile units return to centcom and await further instructions, repeat..."

"In fifty yards, turn right."

"...and await further instructions."

"This is Foxtrot Alpha Whisky, we still haven't gotten through to Toddington services, there's vehicles blocking the service lane and..."

"Turn right."

"...through, it's going to take us at least another fifteen minutes, over."

"Foxtrot Alpha Whisky, this is control, please..."

"In two hundred yards, bear left."

"...I repeat, turn around and head back to base, priority one."

"Acknowledged, control. Foxtrot Alpha Whisky out."

"In fifty yards, bear left."

"Yankee Zulu Tango, please return to base, M1 clearance no longer..."

"Now, bear left."

"...I repeat, M1 clearance no longer a priority, please proceed..."

"At the roundabout, take the third exit."

Jeff felt his heart beat faster.

"...cars traffic, I repeat, all cars traffic, return to nearest base and await instructions..."

What the fuck is going on?

"Now, take the third exit."

Jeff did so, mind racing. 'All cars traffic' had to mean traffic cops, right? They're withdrawing *all* of them? And calling off the M1 units sent to clear the blockage?

"Stay on the road for one-point-two miles."

No traffic cops. So, no one to pull him in. Even if they know about the car.

Even if anyone was still watching the traffic cameras.

Jeff's eyes flicked down to the satnav, and he started stabbing at the screen. *Fuck 'no motorways',* he thought. *Maybe I can still make PMQs.*

CHAPTER TWENTY EIGHT

"In a quarter of a mile, you will reach your destination."

"And what do we fucking do then?" Luke asked bitterly.

"We set the satnav for London. Avoiding motorways."

Luke glanced over at me while I carried on talking. "He came off the motorway to avoid the cameras because he knows we're after him. He's not going to stop heading for London – the protests, PMQs. So, if we set the satnav for central London, when we get to his last known…"

"We should be following the same route he's taking." Hearing Luke speak the same words at the same time as me brought back a memory of holy-shit-was-it-really-still-just-*this*-morning; the police, the paramedics, myself, Kelly, and thirty kids all saying 'Yes' at once. I shuddered.

Luke nodded. "That should work, but we need to know where he's heading as close as possible – these things can take you very different routes, even if your destination is only different by a street or two." He glanced at me again. "Where is he going?"

"I don't know," I said, disappointed. As shit-scary as it was to talk without any control and no notion of what I was going to say before I said it, I'd hoped some part of me would be able to put it together somehow, that my subconscious would be able to filter everything I knew about Jeff and spit out an answer.

And then Luke said, "Okay, what's your best guess?"

I looked at the clock. 11:32.

"My best guess is he'll give up on PMQs – Luton to Westminster in thirty minutes doesn't feel doable, especially only taking A roads. I know he comes over a bit of a hippy, but he's got a ruthless pragmatic streak. So, he'll head for one of the protests. And I'll have to guess he'll go for Freedom From Europe; he hates them so much, I'm sure he'd love to kill a bunch of them, especially like this. He'd probably think it was poetic justice."

"Well, okay then," said Luke. "Put in St James's Square. Avoiding motorways."

I did so, spinning the dial with more ease this time.

***

Jeff tried to shut out the noise from the boot as he reprogrammed the satnav to take him to Junction 10 but screaming had joined the banging. She'd clearly worked out that the car was in an urban setting and saw this as a good chance to draw attention. Jeff found this admirable in the abstract, but intensely irritating in particular.

He allowed that frustration to enter his voice as he yelled over his shoulder, "I am not going to hurt you, but I need the car and I have to get where I am going, and I am not going to let you out until I get there, and I would really, really like you to stop making that noise."

She yelled something that sounded suspiciously like the word "cunt" and carried on banging. Jeff sighed and turned back to the satnav. He punched in Houses of Parliament, turning off the 'no motorways' setting. The device calculated one hour and three minutes. Jeff grinned to himself. On a mostly empty M1? He looked at the clock. 11:34.

It would be one hell of a push.

But it was one fuck of a prize.

"Fuck it," he said, and turned his full attention back to the road.

CHAPTER TWENTY NINE

The journey through Luton city centre seemed to take an age. The A505 was rammed with traffic, and when the roundabout took us to Castle Street and then London Road, roadworks brought us almost to a standstill. I thought about Jeff, somewhere ahead in the dark red Prius, maybe sat on this very road, crawling along. I hoped he was as frustrated as we were. I hoped that would make him do something stupid, but as I thought over what I knew about him, I realised that was pretty unlikely.

Still, I kept picturing the car in my mind; it was odd because I still didn't remember seeing it, but since describing it, I *could* picture it in my mind, and Jeff's odd-yet-familiar bald head behind the wheel.

I willed him to be caught in this, to do something stupid, to slow down.

I willed us to catch him.

***

Jeff *was* caught in the traffic, though his mastery of the Prius's air conditioning meant he was no longer sweating. The banging and muffled shouting was still coming from the boot, however, and that *was* making him nervous. The scanner was telling him that police were being pulled back to local stations, so he supposed he was probably safe from being spotted by some random cop car, but if the wrong have-a-go hero were to get involved...

Also, the clock was ticking.

It was 11:42 when Jeff finally hit the London Road roundabout and got on the M1 Junction 10 feeder lane. He was so focussed on getting up to speed that he didn't see our red Galaxy passing behind him on the roundabout as he accelerated up the slip road.

But I saw him.

***

"Luke, he's on the slip road! He's heading back on the motorway!"

"Fuck!" Luke flipped the indicator from left to right and moved lanes, eliciting an angry honk from the blue Volvo he cut up in the process.

"Please, don't do anything else crazy, okay? We can catch him; he's just pulled on."

"I won't. But why the fuck is he going back on the M1?"

"It doesn't make any sense. Jesus, if I hadn't spotted him..."

"Well, you did." Luke steered us onto the slip road. The traffic was light on the approach itself, most of the stuff we'd been stuck in clearly local lunchtime congestion. Or maybe word was out about the M1 problems.

"Where the fuck is your mate?" The frustration in Luke's voice was palpable.

We'd cleared the on-ramp and were now back on the motorway. I scanned the horizon. "I can't see him. He must be hammering it."

Luke grinned, and this one looked real, if not entirely happy. "Two can play that game," he said, and floored the accelerator.

***

The banging from the boot had stopped as Jeff reached the motorway. He'd floored the accelerator as soon as he hit the slip road and moved over to the fast lane.

He'd just topped one hundred miles per hour when the next bang came.

He felt the rear suspension flex from the blow, and that in turn caused the car to swerve. The steering had a floaty quality Jeff didn't like at all, and he steered into the skid and hit the brakes – fortunately, the centre lane he was drifting into was empty – feeling the ABS kick in, causing the car to judder as his speed bled down to eighty, then seventy.

The car back under control, he willed his fingers to relax from their death grip on the steering wheel, and spoke loudly but calmly, face turned sideways, hoping his voice would carry. "I was driving over one hundred miles per hour when you did that. It nearly killed us both. I'm going back up to that speed again, so if you want to make it out of this alive, maybe stop FUCKING BANGING BACK THERE!"

The yell burned in his throat, his fury suddenly all the way to the surface. He stomped his foot angrily down on the accelerator and swerved back into the fast lane.

The woman in the boot stayed still.

***

We saw the Prius in the centre lane. "Got you, you fucker," muttered Luke as he leaned forward over the steering wheel. Jeff's car accelerated, moving back into the fast lane, and I looked over at Luke. His teeth were bared in a grin-snarl and his eyes were narrowed. The engine noise was a roar. The distance between us and the Prius was closing; slower now Jeff was back up to speed, but we were still gaining.

I looked at our speedometer. One-ten. The car felt to me like it was vibrating in time with the overclocking engine. It made my teeth itch.

Fuck.

"Luke, what are you going to do?"

"I'm going to ram him off the fucking road. This ends here." He spoke through clenched teeth, eyes never leaving the road. Jeff's car had maintained the gap between us, still a good thirty yards ahead. I heard our engine getting louder and watched the speedometer climb to one-twenty. The bland scenery at the side of the road was becoming a blur. The vibration had grown, felt more like a rattle. I tried to speak calmly but had to raise my voice considerably to get over the engine.

"Luke, if you hit his car at this speed, you'll kill all of us."

"Fine by me. End him. Ends you. Ends me. Ends the song."

"Luke, I don't want to die." I wouldn't have known it before I said it, but as soon as it was out, I knew it was true. Despite all of it; the guilt, the horror of what I'd seen, the seemingly bottomless well of revelation at how drastically and permanently my life had changed for the worse – I still wanted to live.

"I don't give a fuck. You deserve it."

The rattling had to be shaking his arms in their sockets, but he kept them clamped to the steering wheel. The speedometer read one-twenty-five. Thirty yards had become twenty-five, was closing in on twenty.

You're about to kill three people!

"Luke, you're going to kill four people!"

Four??

"Four?" He spat the word out, but I noticed the speed drop back to one-twenty. The vibration was still there, but no longer bone-rattling. Again, I had the sensation of the words passing through me.

"Yes, four. There was a baby seat in the car. He put it in the van. The parent must be in the car. Must be in the boot."

"How do you know he didn't just kill the parent? Dump

the body?"

I don't...

"Because he wouldn't. He killed John Cash because he felt he had to and because he thinks killing police is justified," I winced at that, but was compelled to continue, "and he's got no problem with the *song* killing people because he thinks people should be honest anyway – for him, that's ultimately on them, not him. But he wouldn't kill someone he didn't have to, and it would have been just as easy to kidnap the parent – probably easier, actually. And there's no one visible in the car other than Jeff, so they must be in the boot." I was panting by the time I'd finished, the words rushing out at volume.

The speed held. The Prius was twenty yards ahead and surely Jeff would have clocked us by now.

"Luke, you're going to kill one of that baby's parents."

Luke took in a deep breath, held it, then exhaled through his teeth, specks of saliva spraying over the steering wheel. When he spoke, his voice was high, almost a whine. "So, what the fuck are we supposed to do?"

"Follow him. He'll have seen us, but that's okay, maybe. Just keep pace. He'll have to slow once we get to London. We should get a shot at him then. Wherever he's going, he'll have to go on foot eventually."

Luke took another deep breath, and as he did, our speed dropped back down to one-ten. The distance to Jeff's car stabilised at fifteen yards.

"The second that fuckstick is out of that car, I am going to *get* him." The look on Luke's face made me afraid.

CHAPTER THIRTY

The road was virtually empty down to Junction 5 and we convoyed along behind Jeff in the fast lane.

After that, things got scary.

Jeff didn't slow down unless the traffic forced him to, weaving through the increasing congestion, undertaking if the opportunity presented itself, hounding the tails of anyone in the fast lane who didn't move over with flashing lights and horns. Luke sat hunched forward over the steering wheel, mouth a thin line of concentration, trying to keep pace with Jeff, finding his own path through the traffic. I was left watching, stomach twisting, a miserable acidic taste in my mouth. Luke's indifference to his own death, and active pleasure at the thought of mine, seemed to be the only thing I could think of.

Then, at Junction 4, Jeff gave us the slip.

He was belting down the fast lane, maybe a hundred feet in front of us, and he waited until the last possible second before cutting across three lanes of traffic and into the off-ramp traffic, horns blaring behind him. Luke twitched the wheel left and I reached out and grabbed it, aware his intended move would take us into the van alongside us.

The sudden swerve brought us a bare inch from the central reservation, and Luke yelled, "Cunt!" as he straightened the wheel.

"The fucking cunt fucked us! Fuck!" The palm of Luke's hand slammed against the dashboard repeatedly and I felt the car drifting again.

"Luke, I don't want to die."

"I don't care."

"But you do want to stop Jeff."

"And how the fuck are we going to do that, genius?"

I don't know.

But I did.

***

Jeff grinned to himself as he drove towards the roundabout. The scanner was giving out little information now, but whatever was going on, they were pulling all traffic cops and patrol cars. No word about the protests, which was good.

He glanced at the clock. 11:52.

"Satnav, don't fail me now. Maximum GTA," he said, as he pulled onto Edgeware Way, building up speed as he wove through the traffic.

PMQs started at noon, wouldn't finish until 12:30. He still had time.

***

"He's using a satnav. He has to, he doesn't know London that well."

"How do you know that?" Luke was frowning, but at least he'd taken our speed down to a less bowel-loosening eighty.

"He told me once, driving back from a gig in Leighton Buzzard. 'I lived there for two years,' he said, 'but I never drove it, thank fuck. Wouldn't have a clue where to start. Nightmare.'"

"But that was before the song! He could have been bullshitting..."

"No! When Cash and I went to see him, he said the song

hadn't really affected him because he'd always been honest. 'I'm an open book,' he'd said. So..." I grabbed my phone out.

"So what?"

I looked at the clock. 11:53.

"...so, if we can work out where he's going, we can find the route on here..." I indicated the phone as I fired up Google Maps "...and work out where to intercept him."

"You said he was going to St James's Square! The Freedom From Europe thing..."

"No, that was a guess, I didn't know..."

"So how do we work out where he's going?"

I didn't know. I *knew* I didn't know. But I felt... something.

"Ask me!"

Luke glanced over, then back at the road. "Okay, fucking Rain Man, where's he going?"

Not a fucking Scooby, mate.

"House of Commons. PMQs would always be his first choice. He hates politicians more than anything. You should have heard him on breaks at rehearsals. That's why he went back on the M1. Let him make up time, give him a shot."

Luke was nodding. "Okay. So how do we catch him?"

"Simple. I think. I plug Junction 4 to HoC into Maps, that'll give me the route he'll be following. We can get ahead of him, pick a point to head him off."

"Okay. That might work. Read out the directions, let's see if anything jumps out."

I did so, reading out turns and street names. When I got

to the Brent Cross Flyover, Luke yelped with delight. "That's just off Junction 1! We've got the fucker now! We'll get ahead of him, wait for him to pass, tail him, and as soon as he gets out of that car, I can fucking end him." The way Luke said it – the pure pleasure in his voice – made my stomach tighten.

Still, I had to admit, it sounded like a plan.

And I also had to admit, figuring out the way through had been a buzz.

CHAPTER THIRTY ONE

We made it to Junction 1 in ten minutes. Five minutes later, we were sat in Wessex Gardens, the southbound lane of the A41 moving past us in a steady stream of traffic. It was 12:07. I wondered again what Jeff's plan was for getting into the Commons, or if he'd even thought that far ahead.

My thoughts were interrupted by a convoy of army vehicles passing us. Six Land Rovers painted in camouflage colours, followed by fourteen trucks. I could see the seated soldiers in the back of each one.

What the fuck?

I turned to Luke. "Finite?"

He nodded. "I need to make a phone call."

"What about if Jeff comes?"

"If you're right, we're way ahead of him. Anyway, this is important. We need to know where that lot are going."

"So, are you phoning Lena?"

"No, she's no good to us – wherever she is, she'll be part of the Thames Valley pool. I need someone in the Met. Luckily, I know a guy. Now shut up with the questions. I need to think."

I shut up.

I saw colour rise in Luke's cheeks as he tapped a name in his contacts, then held the phone to his ear.

"Hey, Matt! Yes, I know, long time." Pause. "Yes, the weekend training event when we got pissed and ended up fucking like rabbits all night." Pause. "Of course, I remember. I still think about the way you sucked my cock sometimes when I jerk off." Pause. "Yes, I know, Wendy. You showed me the photo of her. From your wedding day. That was before the cock sucking, obviously." Pause. "I just can't help myself, that's the truth. If anyone asks me, I answer honestly. It's exactly like a curse." Pause. "Glad you asked. I want to know where they're planning on putting down the ring of steel once the martial law decree is issued so I can intercept a man who was intimately involved in causing all the deaths that are happening." Pause. "Well, here's the thing. My chances of telling anyone about us are reduced a measurable amount if you tell me what I want to know." Pause. "That's helpful. Have they given you the time?" Pause. "Cool. It's been emotional."

Luke hung up the call, glanced at the clock (so did I, reflexively - 12:10) and turned to me. Whatever my face was doing made him laugh. It was a strange sound, and over quickly, but it still made me feel relief to hear it.

It would be the last time I heard him do it.

"Okay, so PMQs is going to start with an emergency statement - they've run a little late, but it'll be happening now or about now. The army is going to start moving in at 12:30, with the official martial law declaration just after 1:00, once the PM is back in Downing Street. They're going to... fuck!"

Jeff's Prius drove past us, heading south. Luke dropped the car into gear and looked for an opening to join the traffic.

He continued talking as he found a spot and pulled out, four cars behind Jeff. "They're gonna secure the Parliament to Downing Street route first, then move onto surrounding the two protester groups at St James's Square and Trafalgar. Once the formal declaration is made, they'll move in to disperse and move out to secure the rest of the city centre."

"Fuck, that could get messy quick." I tried to blink away

the mental images that were starting to form, looking instead at the route on my phone. "But if Jeff's on the same route as Maps, that won't be an issue – he should head onto the A4200, then down to the Thames. It'll be round the other side of the first deployment."

Luke grimaced. "Good. I want this fucker to myself."

I thought about Jeff, and his hammer, and Officer Cash. But Luke didn't ask me any questions, so I didn't say anything.

CHAPTER THIRTY TWO

Jeff was driving past London Zoo when the banging started again. It was hard enough to affect the suspension, but thanks to the relatively slow pace of traffic, it didn't cause any problems with the steering. He sighed.

"We're nearly there!" He looked at the satnav, then the clock. 12:17. "Ten more minutes. Fifteen, tops. I will let you out. I promise. As soon as we stop."

Silence. Then another thump.

Jeff sighed again.

***

"Did you see that?" Luke asked.

"If you mean the movement in Jeff's car, yes. Looked like he hit something, but he didn't."

I stared ahead. We were three cars behind Jeff now. As I watched, the car lurched again.

"That's the hostage. They're in the boot of the car. Making a pain of themselves." Luke grinned.

"And that's good news why?"

"Well, they're still alive for one, and for two, it's a helpful distraction." We followed Jeff left, then right, the route he took mirroring the display on my phone.

"I think this is working!" I said, excitement driving my pitch a little higher than I'd have liked. "If it is, he'll turn left onto the 501 at the bottom here."

"We'll see," said Luke. The white van in front of us

turned left onto Robert Street. We crept forward. Two cars behind Jeff now. The traffic halted ahead as the lights turned red.

***

"Traffic congestion ahead."

Jeff scowled at the satnav display. The message read 'Reroute? Yes/No.' Jeff shrugged and tapped the yes button. The traffic started moving again. He returned his gaze to the road as the wheel turned on the screen.

"Route recalculation."

***

The timing couldn't have been much worse.

Jeff was sat in the left-hand lane, indicating left. I was concerned about the light change, but confident that with the pace of traffic, the worse we'd run was a yellow.

Then he changed lanes.

Horns blared as he cut up a black cab, then drove across the street, turning right onto the A501.

"The fuck?" Luke stomped his foot down and wrenched the wheel to the right and I heard the tyres squeal in protest. We shot forward, threading the gap on our right with inches to spare, setting off more horns. The black cab that Jeff had cut up was still moving forward, and Luke veered left again, running our car between the lanes before pulling back in and turning right. The light turned from yellow to red as we passed it, and ahead of us, the Prius put on a sudden spurt of speed before taking a left-hand turn, horn blaring.

Luke gritted his teeth and hunched forward. I braced myself against the door with my right arm.

***

Jeff leaned on the horn as he took the turn, hoping any pedestrians using the crossing would take the hint.

The road was wide, two lanes, but the left lane had a lot of parking bays, most of them occupied, and what seemed like a fleet of black cabs on the right were moving too damn slowly – Bill and his mate would be all over him in very short order.

"The speed limit is thirty miles an hour," chirped the satnav.

Jeff glanced over at the wide, pedestrian-free pavement.

"In for a penny," he said.

***

We came around the corner doing forty miles per hour, the car on the edge of sliding, just in time to see Jeff mount the pavement.

"You are fucking kidding me," I said.

"Fuck it," said Luke and turned the wheel left. The bump of going over the kerb shook me in my seat.

We ran the pavement all the way to University of Westminster. Two of the buildings had scaffolding that created a tunnel over the pavement. Jeff lost his wing mirror on the edge of the second one and I heard it crunch under our tyres as we went over it.

Jeff was blowing the Prius horn the whole way, and the handful of pedestrians ran into the relative safety of the road as we shot past them. We were closing in on Jeff, but he was still a good sixty feet ahead of us as we reached the crossroads.

The road ahead was blocked – a heavy yellow police barrier. Unmanned, but solid enough. Jeff tapped the brakes – I saw the lights flash red, like the car was winking at us – and then he was skidding right, heading the wrong way up a one-way street, horn still blaring.

"Fuck you!" said Luke, and sent us into our own skid.

The traffic was parting to either side as Jeff barrelled through and we followed in his wake. He took another sliding turn over a pavement and onto a roundabout with a large park in its centre. I remember seeing a couple standing under a tree, watching us, jaws open in identical expressions of astonishment as this absurd James Bond car chase in sensible family vehicles careened past them.

At the far end, he turned right. It was another one-way street, and we were again going the wrong way, but this one was empty. The end of the road had another empty barricade, but this one had a gap in the right corner between the road and the pavement and Jeff powered through it.

As Luke followed, I glanced down at the map on my phone. "Oh shit, this is Oxford Circus!"

As we entered the road, Luke accelerating to try and catch up with Jeff, I looked around at the street, empty of traffic and with only a small group of people in the street (some looking around at the sound of the engines and scattering to the pavements).

"This is the march route! That's why the barriers, why there's no cars!"

Luke's cheeks twitched in what might have been a smile. "Good. No way the fucker's getting through that to Parliament."

***

Jeff glanced at the rear-view mirror. The red Galaxy was close enough that he could make out my face in the passenger seat. I looked pale and scared. He glanced ahead again. Too many people – the rally should have already started in Trafalgar Square, but there were still groups of people drifting along the protest route. He wasn't going to make it to Westminster.

He gave it one last thought, then let it go.

He could still make the rally.

If he could get rid of the car behind him.

He looked at the police scanner on the passenger seat. He undid his seatbelt and let the car slow down.

***

We were twenty feet behind Jeff when he suddenly jogged right. As he did so, the passenger side door opened, and I saw a large, black object fall from the car.

Luke yelled, tried to turn left, hitting the brakes, but we were going too fast. What I now know was the police scanner momentarily lodged in front of the left wheel, throwing us into a skid before finally passing under the car as we mounted the kerb.

We were going fast enough that when we hit the wall under the window of Hamleys, the glass shattered outwards, showering the front of the car.

The engine cut out.

Then the airbags exploded, pinning us in our seats.

"Fuck!" yelled Luke.

I heard his car door handle flap once, then I saw the door swing open. He moved to get out, jerked back in his seat, cursed again, and started reaching for his seatbelt.

"Fuck," I said wearily, and started reaching for mine.

***

Jeff only made it another few hundred feet. There were too many people now, the drizzle of individuals becoming a crowd. Still, he'd bought himself a big enough lead to get away, he thought. Especially with the protesters – on foot, he could disappear in seconds.

He pulled over, grabbing his laptop bag from the passenger footwell and slinging it over his shoulder as he stepped out of the car. In a movie, he'd have remembered the hammer in the glove compartment, but life isn't a movie, and he forgot it. For all I know, it's still there.

He looked behind him, seeing the red Galaxy parked drunkenly across the pavement, steam rising from the crumpled hood.

Then he saw the doors open.

"Fuck," he said.

Remembering his promise, he pulled the boot release, then jogged towards the crowd, eager to get in among the river of people. His heart was pounding, but he felt good, like a weight was lifting from his shoulders.

Then something hit him around the knees, hard, and he fell on his face.

CHAPTER THIRTY THREE

Luke got out ahead of me. His gait was clumsy at first, and I actually watched him run off a limp, his pace gradually increasing as he favoured his right leg less and less. My face was sore from the airbag, but I was otherwise unhurt. However, my door had initially stuck and by the time I forced it open, Luke had a sizeable head start.

I started running.

I looked ahead, vision slightly impaired by the swaying motion of my run, and saw Jeff moving towards the crowd, head down, stalking fast. Then I saw a woman spring from the boot of his car and charge him down with a spectacular rugby tackle.

I felt a surge of joy in my chest. I ran faster. Luke closed in.

***

"Where's my fucking son, you fucking psycho?"

The woman screamed this in Jeff's ear before smashing him on the back of the head. His forehead bounced off the tarmac and tears squirted into his eyes as the pain burst and spread across his face. He got a brief impression of wild, blonde hair in a cloud around a face scrunched and twisted with anger.

He tried to roll, hoping to force her off him – he could feel her straddling his back – but she lifted her hips, allowing him to turn under her, then sat back down on his stomach, hard enough to wind him.

His reply, "I left him at the services," came out as a whispered croak that was swallowed by the noise of the crowd.

"You sick fuck, where is he?!"

This time, she slashed at his face and he felt her fingernails draw hot lines across his cheek. He waited until the blow had moved past his face, then sat up and pushed forward, his hand grabbing the woman just above her waist. He moved fast and caught her off-balance. His back groaned in protest, but he succeeded in throwing her backward and off him.

***

Still running several yards behind, I saw Luke, sprinting full pelt, get to within feet of Jeff and the woman, then suddenly collapse in a tangle of limbs. My brain took a second to make sense of what my eyes were trying to tell me, but I worked out that Jeff had managed to get the woman off him and in Luke's way. I saw Jeff stand up, straighten his shoulder bag, see me, turn, and run. I wanted to swear but decided to save my breath. I spat and ran faster.

As I started to draw level with Luke, still on the ground, trying to get to his feet, he said, "Don't look back! Just stay on him!"

I fixed my eyes on Jeff's bald head and the ripple he was causing as he pushed through the thickening crowd. I ran faster. I didn't look back.

***

Jeff pushed forward, trying to weave through the protesters, but it was getting harder as he approached the turn to Piccadilly Circus. There were just too many people, and even with his weaving and shoving, he couldn't maintain the same pace. He stole a glance behind him, and couldn't see anyone chasing him, though he knew I couldn't be far behind.

He didn't know central London by car, but he knew this area well enough on foot, thanks to all the big marches he'd been on, down the decades. He felt the ghosts of all those miles, all those causes in his mind, calling up a mental map. Regent Street St James's had a car traffic barricade to mark the edge of the march route, but no police presence. Jeff changed direction, cutting across the crowd.

***

His passage through the crowd was easy enough to track at first; all I had to do was head in the line of pissed off people who had either been pushed past or shoved out of the way. I was also moving pretty fast for me, the adrenaline from the accident surging through my muscles, grateful for the outlet to action.

Then I lost the trail. A huge, pink banner – some union branch, looked like – blocked my view of him, and by the time I'd gotten past it, he wasn't there anymore.

I pushed forward in the direction I'd last seen him moving, assuming he had to still be following the crowd, moving towards Trafalgar Square. As I did so, panic started building, my heart hammering painfully in my chest as the adrenaline from the crash started to wear off. *Where was he?* Up ahead, I heard faintly the sound of amplified music – at this distance, really just a hint of percussion and bass noises.

I pushed my way across the stream of foot traffic, heading for the far side of the road – the crowd was thinner there, and I should be able to see better and make faster progress. The road was wide here, the three-way junction outside of Piccadilly Circus teeming with people. I kept moving in the direction of the crowd, head snapping around, trying to get a bead on Jeff.

I was starting to panic when Luke's yell reached my ears, carried over the conversation of the crowd with ease – a professional necessity, I supposed. "Bill! He's there!" Luke was pointing down the A4201. I couldn't see Jeff, but I didn't waste any time in changing direction. Nor did Luke.

CHAPTER THIRTY FOUR

Jeff was not-quite-sprinting down the street, laptop bag slapping against his thigh with each step. The numbers of people here were tiny by comparison with the march, mainly bemused shoppers heading in and out of St James's Market. He weaved in and out of the people with ease, feeling good, feeling the yards to Trafalgar Square passing under his feet. Straight down to Pall Mall, then left to the square. Ten minutes tops. Bags of time. He'd meet back up with the march at Haymarket, of course, but he'd be way ahead of his pursuers by then.

He started trying to visualise the likely setup of the sound desk, how he might most easily plug in the laptop, how long it would take. If he'd see someone he knew, if that'd help somehow.

He kept moving forward.

He didn't look back.

***

Luke had put on an incredible burst of speed, pulling away from me and closing the distance with Jeff steadily. He was still favouring his right leg slightly and I wondered how much pain he was fighting through.

My own legs were protesting again at the unexpected exercise with an ache that stretched from ankle to knee, snarling at each heavy footstep, but I jogged on, determined not to lose sight of Jeff again.

Luke was maybe fifty feet from catching up with Jeff when the man ran into him.

He'd burst from the gym door, tie flapping loose over his shoulder, mobile jammed to his ear, fast jogging across the pavement. He didn't look in either direction, and Luke didn't stand a chance. He tried, anyway; pivoting on his right foot, allowing himself to spin, but the force of the collision was too strong for him to keep his feet and he went sprawling onto the concrete.

"What the actual fuck, mate?" yelled the man, face flushing red down to his buzzcut roots.

I looked up. Saw Jeff glance back, eyes widening with recognition, then turn forward and put on a burst of speed.

I was too tired to swear. I put on my own burst of speed.

***

The slapping of the laptop bag was getting painful with the increased pace. Jeff slid the strap so it rested against his back, then took the junction at Charles II Street at a dead run, trusting the traffic closures to prevent him being hit. His lungs were starting to hurt and he could feel a stitch developing in his left side, but he kept up the pace, snatching a glance behind him.

He saw me, looking flushed and ill, like I might throw up. Behind me, he saw Luke, the tall man with the broad shoulders, intense brown eyes glaring under a thick, dark fringe, powerful arms moving inside his tight black jumper as he ran, already back up and gaining on both of us.

He was drawing close to the statues now, the three pillars stark against the skyline. He saw some men sitting under them, chatting, and they looked up as he ran past.

Jeff didn't stop. He could hear slapping feet on the pavement, getting closer – Bill's fast friend, he assumed, but didn't look to check, concentrating on trying to find another burst of speed, but it was no good; he could feel his body flagging, his lungs aching with each drawn breath, protesting the twenty-plus years of hand-rolled ciggies and spliffs.

He pushed forward, tears in his eyes, aware that there

was a larger group of people on the road ahead, moving towards Trafalgar Square. As he drew closer, he saw the front row of the march had a huge banner spread across it, held at chest height. It read 'OUT MEANS OUT!'

Then he was hit around the waist, and for the second time in ten minutes, felt himself tackled to the ground.

***

I saw Luke hit Jeff just as I came level with the statues and sighed with relief, slowing to a gentle jog, trying to take deeper breaths. Luke had him and was probably going to beat Jeff to a bloody pulp, and I realised I had no desire to stop him. Jeff had killed a man in front of me, had allowed hundreds more to die, maybe thousands, and had been on his way to kill many thousands more. I found that any notions I had about justice and fair punishments had evaporated – or maybe they'd always been lies I told myself, and I was no longer capable of doing it. Regardless, I found myself calm, even faintly amused, as I saw Luke sat on Jeff's back, punching Jeff on the back of his bald head, smashing his face against the tarmac. Most of all, I felt simple relief. No more running. It was over.

Luke hit Jeff again.

Then the men who had been sat around under the statues reached Luke.

Two of them grabbed him under the armpits and dragged him off Jeff while the other four yelled "Oi, oi!" almost in unison. Luke was thrown forward, and before he could get up, the two who'd thrown him started kicking him, blows coming into his face, ribs, and legs.

I took in the men – green bomber jackets, shaved heads. Black drainpipe jeans tucked into long socks poking from the top of black combat boots. One had a tattoo of the Union Jack across the side of his shaven head.

My stomach turned over.

Two more men had joined in and now all I could see of Luke was an arm, flung out to one side. It jerked with each blow that landed. The sound was like that of a wooden mallet tenderizing a steak.

I saw two others standing over Jeff, asking him if he was alright.

My mind flashed back to *Lord of the Flies*, Piggy and his date with the boulder.

I put my hands in my pockets and started walking, head down, as fast as I could.

I didn't look around. I didn't look back. I focussed on the near horizon, the road with the other marchers in it. The column had stopped, and I stole a glance up. They were watching the beating, faces showing slack indifference with the odd look of amusement. I kept walking, keeping the statues at my back between me and the crowd.

The Freedom From Europe movement march. Moving towards Trafalgar Square and Climate Annihilation. No police because of Finite. Luke, looking like Luke, beating down Jeff, who looked like one of them.

And me. Walking away as fast as I could, trying to look invisible.

I didn't feel like crying or screaming. I didn't feel much of anything except cold, suddenly. The late summer sun was coating the street, but still, I felt a chill that ran right through me.

I could still hear the sound of the beating they were giving Luke, and behind it, murmuring voices; from the men with Jeff, I assumed. All of a sudden, I discovered that I didn't actually care about Jeff, or the song, or stopping anything.

I walked onto Pall Mall, looking ahead the few hundred yards to where the Climate Annihilation crowd was streaming, in all their grubby, multicoloured, ragged glory towards Trafalgar Square, where loud music was playing, and no doubt the usual suspects would soon be speaking, a parade of consciences each voicing their version of King Canute's lament as the tidal wave of history and physics, metaphorical and literal, rolled over them all, there to drown the whole consciousness experiment once and for all.

And I didn't give a shit.

Deep down, I didn't give a shit about anything beyond drawing the next breath, and the one after that, and the one after that. Taking the steps that would lead me away from Jeff and his mission and the men who were beating Luke, and who would no doubt beat me too if they could get their hands on me. I wanted more. More steps, more breaths. Only that. The peace of being alive and in motion.

I'd moved far enough away that I could no longer hear the grunts and smacking sounds from whatever was left of Luke. I cared, but I didn't care. It was over, he was over. I wasn't and didn't want to be. I wanted to live, and I wanted none of his pain.

And when the voice behind me – male, gruff, and loud – yelled, "Oi! Mate!" I didn't hesitate.

I ran.

CHAPTER THIRTY FIVE

It's a hundred and twenty yards from the corner of Pall Mall and Waterloo Place to where the Climate Annihilation crowd were gathered – I know, because I looked it up, after I got here and before they shut down the internet. That hundred and twenty yards brings you dead level with the statue of George III on his horse. By a funny coincidence, one hundred and twenty yards is the length of an American football field, including the ten-yard end zones, so there's plenty of information out there about how fast it can be covered, average speed – or, at least, there was.

Usain Bolt, for example, according to the internet, could run a hundred and twenty yards in somewhere between nine-point-five and nine-point-seven seconds, all other things being equal, whereas an average of seventeen seconds would apply to a fourteen-year-old (according to an anonymous poster on Yahoo! Answers).

I think I was closer to Bolt than the fourteen-year-old.

It was mainly the terror, of course; from behind me, I could hear a clatter of feet so numerous it sounded like a hailstorm, and as I looked dead ahead, feeling energy surge into aching legs coupled with a new looseness around my knees and ankles that felt positively miraculous, I could see the crowd of protesters reacting to what was behind me. There was a ripple of horror, many pulling away, but some others pulling together, faces twisting to anger, clearly intending to stand their ground.

I had time to take it all in, in the however-many-seconds it took me to cover the ground from the turning to the statue; the ebb and flow of the crowd in front of me, rippling like a tide moving in both directions at once. Something flew over my head from behind me. Individual words had become a single wall of noise, an inarticulate expression of rage, of lust for and will to violence, and I fled in front of it, aware with a calm that was unsettling that I was running for my life.

I reached the line of the Climate Annihilation crowd, the people who'd held their ground making space for me. I ran straight through the line and kept going.

I didn't look back.

***

Jeff had joined the charge but got himself out on the right-hand edge, and he found it no trouble at all to peel off there, passing to the right of the King George III statue. He heard the sounds of yelling, grunts, cries, and shattering glass, but he didn't look back.

If the north-west corner of Trafalgar Square was about to turn into a riot, so be it; that should give him a straight shot at the stage on the far side of the square. He swung his laptop bag around and held it to his chest as he ran on, slowing from a sprint to a fast jog.

As he made the turn to the south-west corner of Trafalgar Square, he saw the crowd was already rippling, moving in two directions at once – a large surge away from the corner above him, and a smaller but also clear stream of people moving towards it.

The ones who were fleeing were heading towards the centre of the square, he saw. Towards the stage that was filling the gap between the two fountains, facing towards the National Gallery.

Jeff smiled. This could still work. He jogged towards the barrier behind the stage.

***

By the time I'd made it into the square, most of the crowd were moving with me as quickly as they could, which, even with the density of people, was surprisingly fast. It was almost like being in a mosh pit, suddenly; the surge for the front as the headliners come out. There were pockets of people moving the other way, either alone or in small groups. I saw maybe half a dozen young men pulling black scarves up over their noses and mouths as they pushed against the tide, the crowd parting willingly for them as they were leaving more room for the rest of us. I could also detect a low rumbling, almost on the edge of my hearing. I couldn't tell with the crowd noise if it was coming from the stage – the music had come to an abrupt halt in the last few seconds – or somewhere else. It was deep, and felt as much as heard.

But then the screaming and yelling started in earnest, and this time it was the crowd moving *me*, the crush suddenly painful, my feet skittering across the ground. There was a terrifying moment when we reached the kerb and one of my shoes got caught on the lip. The wrench as the crowd pulled me past was painful, but mercifully, my shoe stayed on.

The noise from behind us sounded like something between a riot and a minor war; yelling, pain, and aggression intermingled; percussive sounds coupled with yells and screams. I couldn't have turned around if I'd wanted to – and, of course, I *didn't* want to – but my heart was hammering uselessly in my chest, my breath starting to feel light and insubstantial.

Then the crowd ahead of me started to thin out. At first, I wasn't sure why, then I realised it was because we'd reached the fountain. A couple of people had stepped into it, but most were trying to find a way round either side. As I watched, I saw a woman with purple hair fall forwards into the water, her legs trapped against the concrete lip by the crush of the crowd behind her. She screamed.

I looked up across the fountain and saw the stage they'd erected between them. Saw, too, the waist-high barricades that had been placed to either side to create a makeshift backstage area, which was now developing into a pretty serious crush point. People were scaling it and there was a steady stream of protesters on the other side heading past the column and across the street, but I could see more and more bodies piling up against it, squeezed from behind, as the mass of movement strained to get away from whatever carnage was happening behind us.

I was close to the edge of the fountain now, and instead of trying to fight past it, I stepped up onto the lip.

As the rumbling sound grew, I had a clearer view of the barrier. I saw it had fallen over on the far side of the stage and people there were moving through the gap easily, but on this side, the crush was building by the second.

I looked again at the smaller streams of folk on the other side, most heading away, some waiting, trying to pull mates over, fighting the weight of the crowd pinning them at the waist. I saw the yellow tabards of security there, too, some assisting the people getting over, others yelling pointlessly for calm, their words swallowed up by the louder shouts of fear and pain.

And behind them, I saw Jeff.

He was strolling along behind the barrier, a few feet back. I noticed his motion first, cutting across the flow of the people fleeing, and then I saw the laptop bag, hugged to his chest.

I felt it then; a surge of hatred. It was cold and black and calming. If looks could kill, he'd have dropped dead. If thoughts could kill, his face would have gushed blood as sure as if he'd told a lie.

I flashed on the noises Luke had made as the skinheads had beaten him. Shame joined the fury, and for a second, I thought I was going to puke.

Instead, I eyed up the front edge of the stage, how many feet it was from the far lip of the fountain.

I felt, for the first time since this strange, long day had

begun, clear of mind and purpose. I knew I would stop Jeff if I could. Not because of the harm he'd do, but because of the harm he'd done to me. He'd hurt me, and I wanted to hurt him back; I knew stopping him would hurt more than anything.

"Will I actually make that jump?" I asked out loud and immediately, the answer came. "Yes, I will."

I smiled as I stepped into the fountain and ran forward as quickly as the water would allow.

***

Everyone was heading away; away from the stage, away from the barrier, away from the square. Jeff watched as the last of the yellow shirts vacated his post by the backstage gate, running to help with the crush.

Jeff stepped through it, walking over to the PA desk he'd spotted behind the stage on the right-hand side.

He whistled the melody from our song as he unslung his laptop bag and placed it carefully on top of the desk. A quick glance told him what he needed – a simple jack to jack, laptop headphones to line in. A cinch. He unzipped the front pouch and located the lead he needed by feel, queuing the song up on the laptop.

***

I reached the far side of the fountain and climbed up on the stone lip. My feet and ankles were freezing, but I barely noticed it. The rumbling had gotten louder still and now seemed to be coming from the south end of the square, the direction the crowd was running in, but I barely noticed that, either. The edge of the stage was maybe four feet away and a foot or so higher than where I stood.

I jumped.

***

Jeff plugged the laptop into the PA, then hit play on the

laptop.

Nothing happened.

He frowned and lifted the laptop, eyes scanning the dials on the desk. It took him a couple of seconds. The main volume was up on the faders, but the line in had a separate dial that was all the way down. He smiled, put the laptop down, restarted the song, then turned the line in volume all the way up.

And that's when I hit him.

CHAPTER THIRTY SIX

As soon as I'd made it onto the stage, I'd spotted the top of his head. When I say I hit him, I mean it; I dropped from the edge of the stage onto his shoulders. His chin connected with the laptop lid as he fell, slamming it shut.

As he dropped to the ground, his body providing a very satisfying cushion for my own fall, the screaming around us grew, as did the rumbling noise, which was now loud enough that I could feel it vibrating through the ground.

Jeff was moving under me, but sluggishly and with no real strength. I reached up for the laptop, pulled the cable out of it, and brought it down on the back of his head as hard as I could. I heard the casing crack and saw the skin on the back of his head split, blood immediately welling up.

I hit him again.

And again.

Then I flung the laptop to one side, knelt up, grabbed him by the shoulders, and rolled him over.

His face was a bloody mess. His forehead was cut and bleeding, his left cheek raw, pink flesh exposed where the tarmac had scraped it, and his nose was bleeding. I pinned his arms at the elbows with my knees. His pupils were dilated, and I wondered if he could see me.

"Jeff? Do you know it's me?"

His eyes were still unfocussed, but he said, "Yes, Bill, I know it's you."

And that's when a voice as loud as God rolled across the square. "THIS IS THE ARMY. YOU NEED TO DISPERSE, NOW."

I looked over in the direction of the voice.

Tanks were rolling up into Trafalgar Square.

Behind them were ranks of soldiers, rifles across their chests, camouflage uniforms incongruous in the city streets.

I watched the crowds who'd just gotten over the barrier trying to get back, piling up. I could hear yelling from the other side of the stage, too; the Freedom From Europe mob still rumbling with the other crowd, I assumed.

I looked back at Jeff. "I don't think this is going to end well, man."

"I agree."

I lay down on top of him, making sure my knees had him pinned. "The laptop is smashed. So, you know you're done, right?"

"Yeah, I get it," he said. His voice was spaced out like he was half-awake and lightly muffled by my chest, but the words were clear enough.

The tanks started rolling forward. The voice boomed out again, ordering the crowd to disperse.

I closed my eyes.

"So, while we wait for this to play out, tell me everything you did after you killed John Cash and left me in your flat."

Jeff started talking.

Shortly after, the soldiers started shooting.

Jeff talked through that, and through them finding us. Jeff was still talking when they loaded us both in the back of a flatbed and brought us here, along with some of the other survivors. By the time we got here, he was finished talking; and I've told you what he told me. Then we were separated. I haven't seen him since.

That was yesterday.

CHAPTER THIRTY SEVEN

As the flatbed pulled out of Trafalgar Square, I saw five thousand, eight hundred and fifty-two bodies; I can't swear they were all dead, but the vast majority were.

The bodies were piled up around the left-hand stage barricade on either side. I saw women and men lying on top of each other, the untidy heap reminding me of an overflowing laundry basket. Further up, in the corner where the riots had been happening, skinheads lay alongside black-hooded men and women, their blood mingling together on the concrete. There were dead children, too. One I saw clearly as the truck took us away; a woman in a rainbow woolly jumper and jeans, lying face down, bullet holes in her back. Over her shoulder, I saw a child's face, somewhere between toddler and infant, blue eyes open and unblinking, staring into the sun, a single, dark hole in the centre of its forehead.

The water in the fountains had turned pink.

Jeff's monologue filled my ears as I took in the carnage. I wasn't really paying attention to him, but, of course, I didn't need to. I heard it then, so I remember it now; that's just how my world is.

Please, forgive my tears.

We were taken out of the city, and we ended up... here. Wherever here is. They asked me if I'd ever dreamt of fucking my mother, and when I answered yes, I was taken inside. Not sure if they use the same test question for women to determine infection – which they're still calling it. I guess even though that makes no sense, it's the only language they have.

I don't know what they did with Jeff.

So yes, I am one of the few survivors of the Trafalgar Square massacre, as it probably won't be called. Because I suspect whoever is in charge now will have very definite ideas about what events need to be recorded in the history books, and that won't be one of them.

The rest of what I've told you, what I didn't see myself or hear from Jeff on the journey here, came from other song victims who have been placed with us; some direct witnesses, others who'd heard the stories from elsewhere. For those of us the song has touched, there's no longer any such thing as gossip or rumour. Word of mouth is one hundred percent reliable.

Another fringe benefit.

I don't know why they haven't caught up with me, yet. Lena isn't here, as far as I've been able to tell, but it's possible they'd hold infected police and soldiers separately. I think it's most likely that my quarantine break just got lost in the shuffle after the deaths at the stadium and in London; and of course, since then, things have escalated even more.

Thanks to Jeff's mate, Derek, and his masterstroke.

The footage was all over social media, at least until they pulled the plug on the internet. No idea if they still have it outside, but... Well, anyway, I saw it on a friendly inmate's phone. He'd managed to get it in somehow, kept it hidden. The guards still don't seem to have worked out that if they want to know if we have a device, all they have to do is ask.

Old habits, I suppose. Or they think what's happened to us *is* catching via contact, in spite of the evidence.

Or maybe there's just too many of us, too few of them.

Anyway.

We know that the poor sod in the visitors' gallery of the Commons wasn't complicit because he told them he'd had no idea it was going to happen until it did, and as he's been exposed to the song...

So smart, though. I wonder if Jeff would have worked it out? Derek couldn't have gotten into the chamber, of course; while his face still hadn't been made public, every copper in the country had his photo as a 'person of interest' in the MK 'attack' by the time midday rolled around. But he figured out he could plant the phone easily enough in the bag of someone who *did* have a visitor pass.

Then all he had to do was wait until the emergency statement was due to start and make the call.

To the phone he'd planted in the visitor's backpack. With the volume set to maximum and the ringtone set to our song.

It was plenty loud enough for the whole chamber to hear it, and just loud enough to be picked up by the microphones in the ceiling, and thereby broadcast to the millions watching at home.

We still don't know how much of the song someone needs to hear to be affected by it, but we do now know that forty-five seconds is more than enough.

We know that because after hearing it, we got to watch as the Prime Minister attempted to resume his emergency statement, only to collapse, bleeding from every orifice in his face.

As far as I know, Derek is still out there, and so's the song; certainly, no one I've spoken to here has seen him, and I've asked around a fair bit. More recent arrivals tell me some of the news media had just started to make a connection between the morning's 'viral music sensation' and the 'Tragic Events in the Commons'. Then they pulled the plug on the TV news, too.

What I think is, it's too late. The truth of how this spreads is simply too unbelievable, so they won't protect themselves against it properly until we're past the point of no return. In fact, I'm sure we're already past it.

An awful lot of people are going to die, and for the rest of us, life is going to be very, very different.

Anyway. That answers your question. And as I'm still trying to build a better picture of this whole mess, I may as well ask you.

How did you end up in here?

END

THANK YOU FOR READING

Thank you for taking the time to read this book. We sincerely hope that you enjoyed the story and appreciate your letting us try to entertain you. We realise that your time is valuable, and without the continuing support of people such as yourself, we would not be able to do what we do.

As a thank you, we would like to offer you a free ebook from our range, in return for you signing up to our mailing list. We will never share your details with anyone and will only contact you to let you know about new releases.

You can sign up on our website

http://www.horrifictales.co.uk

If you enjoyed this book, then please consider leaving a short review on Amazon, Goodreads or anywhere else that you, as a reader, visit to learn about new books. One of the most important parts about how well a book sells is how many positive reviews it has, so if you can spare a little more of your valuable time to share the experience with others, even if its just a line or two, then we would really appreciate it.

Thanks, and see you next time!

THE HORRIFIC TALES PUBLISHING TEAM

ABOUT THE AUTHOR

Kit Power lives in the UK and writes fiction that lurks at the boundaries of the horror, fantasy, and thriller genres, trying to bum a smoke or hitch a ride from the unwary.

He also watches the movie Robocop (The Greatest Movie Ever Made) with friends and records the resulting conversation for your listening pleasure:

https://talkingrobocop.libsyn.com/

ALSO FROM HORRIFIC TALES PUBLISHING

High Moor by Graeme Reynolds

High Moor 2: Moonstruck by Graeme Reynolds

High Moor 3: Blood Moon by Graeme Reynolds

Of A Feather by Ken Goldman

Angel Manor by Chantal Noordeloos

Doll Manor by Chantal Noordeloos

Bottled Abyss by Benjamin Kane Ethridge

Lucky's Girl by William Holloway

The Immortal Body by William Holloway

Wasteland Gods by Jonathan Woodrow

Dead Shift by John Llewellyn Probert

The Grieving Stones by Gary McMahon

The Rot by Paul Kane

Deadside Revolution by Terry Grimwood

Song of the Death God by William Holloway

High Cross by Paul Melhuish

Rage of Cthulhu by Gary Fry

The House of Frozen Screams by Thana Niveau

Leaders of the Pack: A Werewolf Anthology

And Cannot Come Again by Simon Bestwick

Scavenger Summer by Steven Savile

http://www.horrifictales.co.uk

Printed in Great Britain
by Amazon